THE JOY CITY POOL

GLENN BRIGGS

Cover design by Haze Long

ISBN: 978-1-7369323-0-8 (paperback)
978-1-7369323-1-5 (hardback)

This book is dedicated to my mother and father,
Vikitha M Briggs and Glenn L Briggs,
and my Godmother, Barbara J Anderson.

TABLE OF CONTENTS

THE JOY CITY POOL

Chapter 1

Kim

Joy City. A west coast city that fell on the poorer side. It was small enough to never find yourself lost in, but big enough to never feel trapped inside of. There was nothing special about it, no attractions, no real sights to see. Nothing ever came in; nothing ever came out. There was nothing that told people to flee from it, but nothing that drew people into it either. From the outside nothing appeared wrong with the city, but most would agree there was no real reason to pay any mind to it. One could live their entire life never knowing of it, and rest assured they weren't missing anything. It was simply a forgotten location on any map it actually showed up on. Simply serving as a connection point between the cities around it that actually mattered.

It was a place where no one actually wrote their story, they were just one small part of a story written by the city itself, and it was all bad. It was a place where you would probably never see the same face twice, unless you made plans to. No one really spoke to anyone that was stranger to them, they just went about their day, living their own life by the three unspoken rules of the city; live with someone worth dying for, get some money, and stay out the way. Most who inhabited the city followed this code. No one had anyone's back, no one watched over anyone who wasn't their own. If you weren't a member of their small family of three, maybe four, they felt no obligation to care for you as they watched you struggle. People just existed in Joy City. No one really lived their life there, not the one they wanted to live anyway.

No one was held accountable for anything either. Crime went unpunished, sometimes completely unacknowledged. Hardly anything was ever traced back to a culprit. Most felt they could get away with anything so long as they stayed within the city's limits. Those who lived outside would say if you want to get away with anything, do it in Joy City. Theft, vandalism, fraud, whatever, no one would care.

For some, doing dirt is inevitable, sometimes it's the only way to make it. Those who had become so used to doing wrong, they had forgotten how to do right, these were the locals of Joy City. No one's hands were clean.

Down a poorly lit road walked a woman of Korean descent, twenty-six years of age. About five foot six in height, slim, long legs, thin waist, very fit. She had big beautiful brown eyes and brown hair that was bob cut stopping a bit past her shoulders. She had an attractive face but it was blemished with an emotionless scowl that never seemed to fade. Her stare was cold, as if she had no soul. As beautiful as she was, she looked as though she had died years ago. Kim, born and raised in Joy City.

Raised by a couple who had adopted her at the age of six, despite her harsh surrounding area she grew up happy under their care. She was everything to them and they were everything to her, and then one day they were gone, murdered.

Kim was just fifteen, and with no traceable family to take her, she was sent back to the same foster home they had saved her from. She was lost; she didn't know how to keep going. The pain, the disgust, the confusion that plagued her mind convinced her that her life was over. To her she had lost the two people that gave her a chance at a life worth living, this changed her forever.

Dressed in all black Kim walked alone down a road lit only by the amber radiance of street lights and headlights of an occasional passing vehicle. Her head hung low as she slowly footed along. A single thin gold chain dangled down from her neck swaying back and forth. On it hung a small gold charm that read her name in a cursive font. She held a blank stare on her face that communicated she was to be left alone. She was walking with her eyes closed, she knew exactly where she was going, exactly where each step put her. She was in a meditative state, thinking, attempting to find peace and calm.

A beautiful young woman walking alone at night in Joy City. Those who knew of the city and what it was like inside would've called it suicide.

She opened her eyes to see she had arrived at her destination. A twenty-four hour mini mart. Her breaths shortened and her heart rate slowed. She again shut her eyes and took a moment to herself. Standing under the store's neon glowing sign she went completely still, concentrating, focusing, preparing herself, but only for a second. She had done it all before, she had done it for six years now. It had become natural to her.

She opened her eyes, tucked her chain, lifted the hood of her jacket up over her head, and slowly walked up to the store's entrance. It was late, there was only a single car in the parking lot. She could feel her surrounding area, she knew there was nothing to be cautious of. She pushed the door open with her foot and stepped inside. The man behind the counter greeted her with a slight nod.

He was a burly man. His thick grey hair, mustache, and beard told his age. He looked tired as he stood slumped against the counter. His face looked red and there was a noticeable imprint of his arm across his forehead. Kim assumed he'd had his head down on his arms attempting to get some sleep.

She walked up towards the counter and stopped, standing a comfortable ways away.

"Hello, what can I get you?" the man asked.

His voice was dull and hoarse.

"Let me get a pack of the blue," Kim said pointing behind him towards the case of cigarettes.

"You got it," he replied.

Her voice, much opposite of his, was light,

reflecting that of a typical valley girl.

The man turned around to grab the small box. He looked slightly to his left out the store's window and frowned.

"Did you walk up here?" he asked.

Kim nodded.

"You must not be from around here. Walking these streets this late at night, they get pretty dangerous," he said over his shoulder.

"I'm not worried about it," she responded.

The man shrugged as he turned back around, resting the box on the counter.

"Just be careful." he added, "Anything else?"

"Yeah actually, could you tell me where the nearest grocery store is?"

"This late at night? There's really only one open and it's pretty far, you don't wanna walk that in the dark."

"It's fine. I'll make it, consequences of working late nights I guess."

The man shrugged again.

"Keep down this street, turn right when you get to Tyndall and then keep straight until you see East Seventh Street. It'll be right on the corner, on foot it'll take you about forty-five minutes."

"Thank you," she nodded.

"Seven ninety-nine," he said, gesturing toward the box of cigarettes.

Kim reached around to her back pocket.

"Working late nights huh?" the man said, eyeing around the store, "I know how that is."

Kim froze in place hearing this. She seemed

thrown off by the man's attempt to make conversation. She studied him up and down for a brief moment.

"Yeah?" she asked.

She had paused with her hand still tucked in her back pocket.

He nodded slowly in agreeance.

Kim's body suddenly shifted. She became noticeably more relaxed than she had been when she walked in. She let her shoulders down, spread her feet apart into a more comfortable stance, and shifted all her weight to her right side. The man took notice to this as his eyes opened a bit.

"Really?" she asked again.

Kim cocked her head and arrogantly grinned in the man's direction. She then took a few steps closer to the counter and swiveled her head around the store as if about to tell the man a secret.

"Do you really?"

Her voice still hushed.

She leaned in close, her upper body hovering over the counter top. The man leaned back slightly taken off guard by her sudden shift forward.

Still grinning, Kim cut her eyes at the man and tilted her head more. She continued staring deep into his eyes. The closer she inched towards him the more he leaned away from her. He was scared, she could feel it. His eyes had grown wide, his breaths had gotten heavier, his entire body had gone stiff. She knew she had him.

She let out half a giggle relishing in his fear

and whispered to him, "Tell me.... you ever killed anyone?"

"What? N-n-no," the man choked, obviously startled by her question.

Kim closed her eyes and shook her head in disappointment. She leaned back from over the counter and scoffed in disapproval of his answer.

"Then you don't know anything about working late nights."

Kim's grin faded. The man was speechless.

"It changes you," she added.

The dead stare she had walked in with had now returned. She pulled a gun from behind her back and shot the man right between his eyes. He dropped to the floor dead.

She leaned back over the counter looking at his body, but only for a brief moment. She then let her focus drift around the store until she found a security camera in the back corner. She twisted her lips into a slight frown and rolled her eyes as she casually walked towards the door.

She grabbed a small handkerchief from her pocket and wrapped her hand in it. She opened the door and slipped outside. Unphased by the murder she had just committed, because it was only the most recent murder of several in the past six years.

Kim is a parent by the minute, a worker in an office by the day, and an assassin by nightfall. This was where she found herself ten years after the murder of her parents. This was her life.

She would now walk a mile in the dark to the only grocery store still open past midnight. She had a daughter to feed.

Chapter 2

Helena

"Ugh…" Kim moaned in disgust.

She was changing her clothes inside the bathroom of the grocery store. She had become sticky from walking in the night's humidity.

As she arrived at the store she pulled a thin turquoise jacket and a pair of black sweatpants trimmed in pink off the rack, headed to the bathroom, and slipped them on. She exited the bathroom with the black hoodie and leggings she had been wearing on hangers. She hung them on the rack in place of what she had picked up and kept moving. She was a cold blooded murderer, the crime of theft had become petty to her.

She slowly made her way through the clothing section of the store, occasionally stopping, pretending to show interest in what she was looking at.

"Need any help finding anything ma'am?" a young female floor worker asked.

"No thank you, just browsing," Kim smiled, looking back at the girl.

Everything about Kim made her perfect for what she did in the dark, easily forgotten, already forgotten by most.

She strolled around a bit longer attempting to appear as natural as possible. Occasionally stopping and removing a shirt from its shelf or rack, viewing it for a few seconds only to eventually lay it back in its place.

She came upon an abandoned cart that held a few socks and shirts in it. She removed them and claimed the cart for herself.

She began moving up and down each aisle, filling her cart with toiletries, snacks, drinks, and canned and frozen foods. She bought things in bulk as she hated being out. She would attempt to limit the number of trips she had to make by buying more than she needed at a time. Her day job provided her with enough for her to spend whatever she pleased on groceries. This was not because it paid so well but because the paycheck she received from her day job was used only for groceries. This check, however, was miniscule in comparison to what she received from a single completed contract as an assassin. She didn't need the day job; she only maintained it as a cover up.

After spending about an hour maneuvering around slow moving shoppers, flashing dozens of fake smiles at people passing by, and pulling what seemed like one of everything from every shelf, she looked over the cart, and declared herself finished. She had packed the cart full enough to be rung up for multiple hundreds of dollars.

She was ready to head to checkout when her cell phone began buzzing in her pocket. She pulled it out and looked at the caller ID. It was her daughter Cindy. Kim adopted Cindy from the same foster home her parents had adopted her from when she was twenty-one and Cindy was ten. Kim thought she would be sound asleep at two a.m.

"Hello?" Kim answered puzzled.

"Uhhh hey…. where are you?" Cindy asked.

Her normally soft voice was very dull and groggy. Kim could tell she had just woken up.

"I'm…. at the grocery store?"

"It's like two in the morning?" Cindy pointed out.

Kim handled most her assassination contracts after dark. Killing was easier after the sun went down. Running errands afterwards was just one way to kill two birds with one stone. But, of course, to someone who didn't know what she had been doing out so late in the first place, grocery shopping past midnight seemed strange.

Kim kept her work as an assassin secret from Cindy which had never posed too difficult of a challenge. Cindy was naturally pretty dismissive about most things and hardly ever overly curious. Kim wanted her to live as normal a life as she could regardless of how abnormal her own was. She usually snuck out after Cindy went to sleep and crept back into the house before she woke up the next morning.

"I was up, and I couldn't sleep so I just started driving and well…. we needed some stuff anyway. Wait, why are you awake?" she asked.

11

"I couldn't sleep either so I was gonna make some tea. Then I saw you weren't in your room."

Kim pressed her lips together, closed her eyes, and blew air out her nostrils furious at herself, remembering that she had forgotten to close her bedroom door before leaving.

"I'm sorry, I didn't mean to scare you, but I'll be home in about half an hour OK? I'm glad you called actually, we're almost out of tea so I'll bring some home and I'll fix us both a glass."

"Alright...." Cindy said.

Her tone told Kim she was suspicious of her late night errand run. She quickly ended the conversation to keep her from attempting to pry any answers out of her.

"Alright I'll see you in a bit. Love you."

"Love you too."

Kim hung up the phone and shook her head in disappointment. She hardly ever made big mistakes when it came to hiding her work, but she knew the little mistakes would be the ones that would start raising eyebrows and questions. *Gotta be better* she thought to herself.

She turned around and headed towards the back of the store where the tea was stocked. She was nearly the only person left in the store, only a few midnight shoppers and store employees still wandered around. When she got to the very back of the store she was completely alone. It was eerily quiet, only air rushing through the rafters above her could be heard. She grabbed the largest box of plain natural tea and rested it on top of her full cart.

Just as she began to make her way towards checkout, a sharp pain hit the front of her head. It started small but rapidly began growing. She put both of her hands on her head and bent over wincing. The pain quickly became worse and worse. She squeezed her head in between her hands as the pain got more and more intense. She let out a small whimper and braced herself against her cart.

She was suffering, struggling to even stand. The pain was immense. She fell to her hands and knees. All her muscles went weak, her heart started pounding, her body began heating up, and she broke out into a sweat. She began letting out disgruntled moans to be heard by no one but herself. She pressed her nails into the floor beneath her and scratched at the slick tile leaving faint marks.

She began taking deep breaths, breathing in and out of her mouth slowly. This was far from normal; she had never experienced anything like it before. Just as she began to panic, the pain began to subdue, slowly fading away.

Still on her hands and knees Kim looked up to ensure no one had witnessed her collapse to the floor. She was drenched in sweat. She dusted off her hands and used her sleeve to wipe her forehead dry. When she pulled it back, she saw it wet with perspiration. Her heart rate began returning to normal as well as her breaths back to their regular pace.

She slowly pushed herself back to her feet panting. Her strength, her balance, her breath, all seemed to come back in a mere instant after the massive headache departed. She was shook, unsure of what she had just endured. Brushing herself off, she looked around again to ensure no one had been watching.

Having no better answer for it she wrote the happening off as a buildup of stress. She couldn't imagine what else it could have possibly been. Placing both hands on her cart, she slowed her pace as she began moving down the aisle once more.

She took notice again to how quiet it was. No one screaming in her ear to do this or that, no one asking anything of her. These were the only moments of peace she had in her life. Juggling an office job, being a mother, and constantly having to watch her every move in order to keep her secret took a toll on her.

Every day she got up, did whatever she had to as a parent, went to work, killed when she was asked to, went to sleep, and repeated the cycle the next day. She had done this for six years. She of course had asked herself many times before if it was time to look for change. She wanted to but simply didn't know how or where to look. Plus, anytime she convinced herself it was time to make a change, something else told her no, that her life was her life and no part of it was to change, ever. She felt trapped. No longer enjoying life but just living it against her will.

She closed her eyes and took a deep breath letting her mind wander. Doing this had always been her way to force herself to relax, unwind, and find the peace she needed in her life. If she could block out her own conscience and the opinions of others and just allow herself to choose the life she would like to live with no outside influence, she believed she could make that change.

But this was a mistake she too often made. Thinking about change with her eyes closed made it impossible for her to see the changes happening right in front of her.

"Uhhh…. hey?!" A small voice cried.

Kim quickly opened her eyes as her cart shook and came to a halt. She looked down to the other end of the cart and saw a girl sitting in front of it looking up at her. It looked as if the girl had been kneeling down, perhaps looking at something, and Kim had run into her.

"Oh my god, I'm so sorry, I didn't even see you there. Are you OK?" Kim asked.

She quickly rushed around the cart and helped the girl up from the floor. She said nothing and just stared at Kim in amazement.

"I'm so sorry, are you hurt?" Kim asked again.

Still the girl said nothing; she looked Kim up and down as if starstruck. Kim then froze herself, unsure of what was happening. They both stood examining each other for a second in what to Kim, was one of the oddest exchanges she had ever been a part of.

Suddenly the shock on the girl's face transformed into the biggest smile Kim had ever seen in her life. The girl lunged forward at Kim with her arms extended.

"Kim!" she shouted, "Oh my god, good to see you girl! How are you?!"

Kim, startled by the girl's sudden movement

had placed her hand on her hip ready to pull a weapon she kept on her at all times; a purple hair pick that had a hidden retractable blade on its end.

"What?" Kim asked, looking at her.

"How are you?" the girl repeated, "It's been a while huh?"

The girl was so confident in her words, so confident in who she was talking to. Yet Kim had no idea who she was.

"I think you have me confused with someone else," Kim told her.

"What? No?" she laughed, "I know it's you."

Kim took a good look at the girl in an attempt to spark some remembrance of her. She was slightly shorter than Kim and looked to be in her late teens. She was skinny, petite, and very pretty. She had long dark blond hair that went all the way down her back, big green eyes, and a smile that just wouldn't go away. Over a black sports bra, she wore a very loose fitting, sleeveless top that read, "I WILL BITE YOU" in all capital letters on the front. She had on a pair of jeans that looked to have been cut with scissors and came not even halfway down her thighs, a pair of black socks that came up to her calves and flat red sneakers. She wore several wrist bands on both her arms along with a string necklace with a single brown feather hanging on the end of it. On her head she wore a black beanie with the words "LIVE FREE" written on it in bold white lettering. She also had a huge red rose tattooed on her right shoulder.

Essentially the girl looked and dressed as if she were Cindy's age, leading Kim to believe even more she had to have her confused with someone else.

"I'm sorry, I don't believe we know each other."

The girl looked at Kim puzzled.

"Kim, it's me," she said, pointing to herself, "Helena?"

"I'm sorry the name doesn't ring a bell," Kim said shaking her head.

The girl laughed at this.

"Eh, don't worry about it, doesn't matter." she giggled, "So how are you?"

"Uhhh…. fine…" Kim said as she walked back around to her cart, "look I'm sorry I gotta…"

"You're lookin good," she interrupted.

"…. thank you?" Kim said with a look of uncertainty.

Kim began trying to move around her but the girl jumped in front of her. She stepped up on the bottom rack of the cart leaning over the groceries inside.

"Ummm…. excuse me…" Kim cried, now getting slightly annoyed.

"So, how's work been?" the girl asked.

"Can you please get off my cart?"

The girl leaned further over the cart with her hands tucked under her chin. The whole time she kept a smile on her face.

"Still doin it huh?" she asked.

"What is wrong with you?" Kim asked.

"I'm just askin about work Kim?" she smiled.

"Work sucks. I go in, sit at a desk, and send emails all day, now can you please move? I need to go," she said attempting to shake her off.

"Not the boring job, the other one."

"Other one?" Kim froze.

"Yeah, the other one," she repeated still holding her smile.

Her voice was so innocent. Kim cut her eyes and looked around confused. *Surely she couldn't know* she thought.

"What other one?" Kim asked.

"What you did at the mini mart about two hours ago?" she said raising an eyebrow.

Kim's heart began to beat a little faster. In her line of work anonymity was a priority at all times. She couldn't afford for anyone to know, especially a stranger and someone who seemed as off as the girl did.

"I don't know what you're talking about," Kim told her.

"What?" the girl laughed, "You put a bullet right between that dude's eyes, what do you mean?"

She jumped down from the cart and walked around to Kim. With a quick swipe she pulled Kim's hair pick from her waist.

"Looked like for a second I was about to be next," she grinned as she extended the blade out.

Kim quickly grabbed it from her and wedged it back between her waist and the sweatpants she was wearing.

"OK, who are you?" Kim demanded.

The girl looked at Kim as if surprised by her question.

"*Helena*? C'mon Kim, keep up," she repeated

again snapping her fingers in front of her face.

She acted as if they had known each other for years. She showed no emotion other than the joy of seeing Kim again. Yet, Kim still couldn't remember ever having seen her before in her life.

Kim was put off by the girl's giddy disposition and something about her made her uncomfortable. Somehow a teenage girl knew her and her secret, yet, she didn't seem emotionally phased by it at all, as if it weren't a big deal. She even somehow knew she had a blade on her. Kim was absolutely thrown.

"How old are you?" Kim asked.

"You feelin OK, you're acting kinda strange, askin a lot of questions," she said, dramatically tilting her head to the side, "that's not like you K."

Kim could only look at her more confused.

".... I need to go..." she said slowly backing away.

"OK, well, tell Cindy I said hey."

Kim's eyes grew wider.

".... right.... Cindy," Kim trembled.

The girl knowing about her seemed strange enough, but she knew about Cindy too. Kim was beginning to get worried. It was unsettling how much she seemed to know.

"Hey, if you're free tomorrow we should grab dinner, I'd say lunch but I know you gotta go collect your money for tonight so maybe uhhh.... seven-ish? Meet me at the statue in front of the mall and we'll go from there?" she cheesed.

What the girl knew was giving Kim a cause for pause; she knew too much for Kim not to know her at all. As much as she hated to go out, especially in the company of others, she needed answers. She wanted to know who the girl was and how she knew all she knew. Maybe talking with her more would jog a few memories of where they knew each other from. If worse came to worse she would have to kill the girl to keep her secret safe. She was fine with either.

"Sure…" Kim nodded slowly.

She backed up slowly dragging the cart out of the aisle staring at the girl as she stared back smiling. She reversed so far she ran into a store employee causing him to drop the several boxes he was carrying. Kim turned around quickly and apologized.

"I'm so sorry, here let me…" Kim froze as she looked back up. The aisle was empty and the girl was gone.

~

Early the next day Kim walked down a quiet dead end road. Careful of each step, she made sure she wasn't being followed or watched. As she came to the end of the road she veered left and cut through the woods. A discreet path existed, one that if a person didn't know was there, they would miss entirely. Kim walked the narrow path, high stepping over tall shrubs and pushing hanging branches aside until she came to a small opening in the path where an abandoned pool hall stood.

The building looked to be in awful condition. The windows were boarded up, the front entrance was nailed shut and the small building was nearly completely consumed by green life. Moss, fallen branches, and weeds draped over each side giving the place a spooky visage. A small mural of a billiards table had been painted on the front of the building. Its faded colors showed the buildings age and only small portions of the scene were still visible from chips in the paint.

It looked to be a place forgotten, sentenced to deteriorate under the plant life swallowing it whole. However, like many things in Joy City, there was more to the old pool hall than what a first glance told.

Kim was not the only assassin in the city. In fact, she was only one member of a small team of assassins. The Pool was what they called themselves, and the old abandoned pool hall played the role of their haven.

From the outside, the building looked like it hadn't been occupied in years. Though inside, it had power, running water, and air conditioning throughout. All these utilities had been tapped and stolen from nearby establishments and set up so that the consumption of the power the building used was untraceable and went unnoticed. The pool hall wasn't much but it didn't need to be, in fact, it worked better for them that it wasn't.

Kim circled around the building to the back entrance. She pulled a large heavy door open and stepped inside. A cool gust of air greeted her upon her entrance. The pool hall was quiet. Two billiards tables with folding chairs positioned around them sat in the middle of the room. A few papers and manila envelopes rested in the middle of each table. The hum of two small flat screen TVs mounted onto the walls were the only sounds she could hear. She remembered so vividly her first time walking into the pool hall; it was different then, much duller.

"Kim, in here!" a deep scratchy voice summoned her from a room in the back of the pool hall.

She entered the room which was lit by only a single lamp that rested on a desk. Behind the desk sat Terrance.

Terrance was a heavy set black man well into his forties. His hair was braided into cornrows and his mustache and beard were finely groomed. Nothing about him was welcoming, not his permanent scowl, his deep threatening voice, or his bloodshot eyes.

"Thought I'd be seeing you today," he said adjusting a pair of reading glasses.

He was shuffling through several papers spread out on the desk in front of him.

"You owe me forty grand, of course I came."

He looked up at Kim and smugly smiled.

"Always about your money...." he mumbled.

"I got a daughter to feed. I can't afford to be doing this for free."

"Well.... we ain't got it yet."

"They didn't pay?"

"Not yet, don't sweat it though it'll come through by tomorrow."

"And if it doesn't?" she asked raising an eyebrow.

"Then they'll be dead by Monday morning."

Terrance was the oldest and one of the founding members of The Pool. He was also the engine that kept it all running. He took all the contracts, assigned them to Kim and the others, and then collected the payments from their clients. Kim didn't quite know the extent of all he did to keep everything running smoothly but she knew it was a lot. He was usually always at the pool hall thumbing through paperwork whenever she happened to show up.

While his exterior appeared cold and hard, deep down he was a thoughtful and caring person, and he loved Kim and the rest of The Pool members like they were his own. However, he always had a bit more of a sweet spot for Kim.

"You good though right? I know you ain't broke."

"No, I'm fine, but I do need to talk to you."

He lifted his head, giving Kim his full attention.

"I don't know about this anymore," she told him.

Terrance sighed and shook his head. He knew where she was getting at.

"Kim, listen…"

"No look," she said, cutting him off, "it's not me. It's for Cindy."

Terrance rolled his eyes.

"I'm already not the best parent in the world but now that she's getting older, I just feel like my priorities aren't in line. I'm missing her grow up cause my mind's on other stuff, and keeping up this facade and trying to hide everything and.... I just don't know anymore."

Terrance took off his glasses and set them aside.

"Kim, in the six years you've been doing this nothing has happened. In the five you've had Cindy nothing has happened. She's been fine because you've done your part to keep her fine. None of what you do has affected her negatively, so why, why now have you been so stuck on this lately?"

Kim couldn't answer. She just sat motionless, staring into her lap. They'd had the discussion several times in the recent months. Kim wanted out of The Pool. She was worried if she didn't break free of the life she lived soon that it would eventually trickle down and impact Cindy in some way, and that terrified her.

"Kim, is there something you're not telling me? Are you OK?"

"Yeah.... I'm fine," she said, in a melancholy tone.

"Then what's the problem?"

She heaved a deep sigh.

"Nothing I guess..."

"Alright then, stop stressin over nothin."

A long pause came between them. Kim regretted opening her mouth and just stared silently into her lap.

"You know they'd want you here right?" he said.

Kim looked up at him staring daggers.

"Don't do that," she begged him.

"They would've eventually told you and you'd have probably ended up here anyway."

"You don't know that," she objected, cutting her eyes.

"When your father gave you that pick, you were six years old, he knew there was a blade in it, that wasn't a mistake. What do you think he meant for you to do with that?"

She again had no answer.

"Kim," he huffed, "Cindy is fine, she can live fine with you doing what you do, kids in this city grow up just fine with all types of parents raising them. I mean look at you, you turned out fine."

"Fine? This is what you call fine? Look at me, I kill people for a living, this is fine? I don't want this life for her."

"OK, then it's simple, don't tell her and she'll never know."

Kim had nothing else to say. He was partially right, as long as she never knew about it, she couldn't be sucked into it. She just feared her own involvement spilling over to her.

"Alright," Kim said as she got up from the chair.

"Alright? We good?" he asked.

"Yeah."

He could see it in her face, she wasn't content, but he let it go.

"Where you headed to?" he asked, putting his glasses back on.

"Just home to get some rest, I got plans tonight.... which reminds me, do you know a

Helena?"

"*Helena*? Nah, who's that?"

"Some girl I met yesterday, it was really weird, like, she knew my whole life but I couldn't recall ever having met her before."

"Your *whole* life?" Terrance asked, leaning forward in his chair.

He was adamant about everyone in The Pool keeping the secret from those not inside. Anyone on the outside that they believed knew anything was considered a target. However, Kim was more curious than she was worried about her; she was just a teenage girl after all. She chose not to tell him that the girl seemed to know she was an assassin.

"Not everything," she assured him.

She had a desire to know who the girl was and how she knew so much. She at least wanted to speak to her again before Terrance called for her head.

"Well nah, I don't know the name, be careful though. Don't take lightly to people knowing your business."

"Probably just an old friend from school I forgot."

"Maybe."

"You here all day?" she asked.

"All week," he corrected her, "Stop by tomorrow I'll have your money."

"Alright."

"Be safe out there," he reminded her.

"Always," she responded.

As bad as she wanted out, she felt trapped. She couldn't see leaving The Pool especially after being a part of it for so long. Yet she remained terrified of Cindy ending up like her. She wanted to be the happy go lucky girl she once was but for now she would remain a killer, a title she longed to shed.

~

Kim stood struggling in front of her bathroom mirror with an earring. It had been a while since the last time she had put on a pair, the hole in her lobe had almost completely closed up. Her days of trying to look cute when she left the house were long in the past, but she wanted to appear as normal as possible meeting with the girl.

"Where are you goin?"

Kim turned around from the mirror and saw Cindy leaning against the doorframe.

Cindy was a petite girl even for her tender age of fifteen. Her skin tone was fair which contrasted with her brightly dyed pink hair she had twisted into two long braids that fell down her back.

"Out with a friend," Kim said as she turned back to the mirror.

Cindy didn't question much but she was sharp. Usually she could tell when Kim was lying or holding back the truth.

"Since when do you have friends?"

"I have plenty of friends," Kim rolled her eyes as she continued struggling with the earring.

"Here."

Cindy walked over, took the earring from her, and motioned for her to bend down. She easily put it

27

and the other in. Kim turned around and looked in the mirror.

"Thanks.... uhhh.... I'll be back later," Kim told her as she slipped past her.

She grabbed her keys, walked out the bedroom, and started quickly down the stairs. Cindy slowly trailed behind her.

"Uhhh.... yeah I hope so, cause I haven't eaten yet so..."

Kim stopped at the bottom of the stairs and cursed under her breath. She always kicked herself for being so forgetful when it came to her responsibilities as a parent.

"I'll be back before eight. I'm just gonna be up the road at the mall, I'll call you and pick you up something on the way back OK?"

"Alright," she mumbled dragging herself back upstairs.

She seemed depressed, it broke Kim's heart. She hated having to always leave her home by herself, she would have liked to have spent more time with her, but time just never seemed to be on her side. Kim was hardly ever home and when she was, she was resting in between working. This was why she wanted so bad to break free from The Pool, to be a better mother and have more time to spend with Cindy. However, leaving behind what kept her stable for the last six years wasn't as easy as she would have liked it to be.

~

Kim arrived at the mall and looked over to the statue of a man riding a horse, the place where she had agreed to meet Helena. She arrived there four minutes past seven expecting to see Helena waiting for her, but she wasn't there. She got out the car and double checked the time on her phone. She had said seven-ish the day before. She assumed that meant right at seven.

She sat there for another five minutes waiting, watching as cars and people passed by. As five minutes turned into ten, she began to get irritated.

I don't have time for this she thought to herself.

Ten minutes eventually turned into fifteen and she had grown tired of waiting. She stood, but just as she was about to walk back to her car a purple painted car with red and yellow flames detailed on the sides pulled up next to her with the radio on full blast. The window rolled down and a voice bearing a heavy Hispanic accent called out to her from inside.

"Kim?!"

From the voice she immediately recognized the person inside, the youngest member of The Pool, Pedro. She rolled her eyes and approached the window.

Pedro was a small built man about the same height as Kim, a bit heavier in weight, but a year or two younger. His hair was cut very low making him appear nearly bald. He also had a messy goatee which Kim and the rest of The Pool members always gave him a hard time about.

Kim had trained and worked very closely with him since he joined The Pool about two years ago.

She was the oldest and most experienced, making her the best choice to train him. They had completed several contracts together over the past two years, basically becoming partners.

"Could you be anymore obnoxious?!" she shouted, leaning into the car window.

"You like the new whip?!" he asked, "Just pulled it out the shop today!"

"Turn the music down!" she shouted.

He silenced the music.

"What's up, whatchu doin out here alone?"

"Just kinda out here..." she said.

She didn't want to tell him the truth because she knew he wouldn't believe her. He knew how introverted she was, he wouldn't believe she was waiting for someone. She also wasn't so sure she wanted him to know that she was anyway.

"What are you doin here?" she asked him.

"Me and the boys were hanging out tonight, I was bout to head home and I saw you sittin there. I didn't think you made your way outside unless you were on contract."

"Just had to pick up some stuff..." she told him.

His facial expression showed he was intrigued by her response.

"Hmmm.... where's the stuff?" he asked with a smug grin.

Kim put her tongue in her cheek, embarrassed being caught in such a silly lie.

"Did you want something Pedro, or are you just saying hi?" she asked ignoring his question.

"Yeah," he leaned over the center console and pushed the passenger door open, "hop in, we gotta talk."

Kim hesitated for a second. She didn't really want to tell him her business but she knew he was one to speculate and pry for until he was given an answer he was satisfied with.

"OK look, I'm actually waiting for someone right now."

"Who?" he asked.

She looked back at the statue and all around the parking lot and sighed.

"You know what, never mind," she said shaking her head as she slid into the car.

Pedro parked in a nearby spot and turned off the car's engine. He pulled a few pieces of paper from the side of his door and tossed them into Kim's lap.

"A contract came through today with a six-figure ticket on his head right here in the city."

Kim picked up and handed the papers back to him without even looking at them.

"That's great, good luck," she said.

"Good luck?" he asked, looking at her confused, "Whatchu mean good luck, we're partners right?"

"I think I'm about done with all this, I don't want this anymore," she said, staring out the window.

"Kim, what's goin on, you good?"

"No, I'm not. I kill people for a living. Ten years ago I'd have believed myself to be dead in my grave before I believed I'd be putting people in theirs."

"Kim, so would I but..."

"But do you have a kid?" she interrupted.

Pedro sunk back into his seat.

"I've had nights where I've taken people's lives, had my hands soaked in blood, and then came home and cooked dinner for Cindy with those same hands, pinched her cheeks with those same hands. I've watched people take their last breath because of what I've done to them and have had to come home and pretend I'm just a regular person working a regular job."

"So what's the problem, if you've done it for six years why can't you do it for six more or ten, why's it bothering you now this many years into it?"

"It's always bothered me, realistically this life sucks."

"I like it," he smiled obnoxiously, "I get a five-figure check every two weeks or so and I get to rid the world of some of its worse people, it's a nice life I'd say."

"But we're not super heroes Pedro, we're assassins. We're not killing bad people, we're just killing people, regular people. I killed a man because he wouldn't give one of his employees a raise. He had ten grand put on his boss' head cause he said no to a thousand-dollar raise. That doesn't even make sense. Pedro that man had a family, and I killed him, over a thousand dollars. This city is awful, I don't just want out The Pool, I want out of Joy City."

"All this is just now getting to you?"

Kim scoffed at his question. She didn't believe

he was listening.

"In the time I've been doing this I've seen everything, you know, you've been there for a lot of it, it's gotten old. The money was great at first but I have enough now to have retired yesterday if I wanted to. Money is what it is but having a body count to show for it is nothing to be proud of, at least not to me."

"Your folks…"

"Ugh, Pedro stop please, I'm so tired of y'all doin that."

"Kim, are we wrong though?"

"What parent would want their child to be a part of this, to see the things that being a part of this puts in front of you?"

"Yeah but, it's practically a family business…"

"I don't care, I think I'm done…. seriously, I think I'm gonna tap out of it."

Pedro sighed over her insistence. He knew he couldn't change her mind. He had gotten to know her well over the past two years and one thing he knew for certain was how stubborn she could be. Once her mind was made up, there was little anyone could say to change it.

"You talk to Big Dog yet?" he asked.

"His name is Terrance," Kim corrected him.

"Did you talk to him?" he asked again

"Tried, he just reels me back in every time. Truthfully, I owe him a lot, he did a lot for me after I lost my parents. When I'd run away from my foster home he'd always let me crash at his place, make sure I had food and everything, he took care of me.

Him and my dad were like brothers. Growing up he was always around, he was basically like family, so it's hard to just leave knowing without him I'd have been sleeping on the streets a lot of nights. But for me, for Cindy, I really think I need to."

A tear formed in Kim's eye that she caught before it began to roll down her cheek. Pedro put the papers back in the door and nudged her.

"Hey, don't do that. It'll be fine, you know he's not gonna force you to do anything you don't want to. We'd all hate to see you go but if you have to to be happy, do it. He'll respect your decision, you know he loves you, he's got your back."

"It's just hard cause…"

"Just talk to him, like really talk to him. Be adamant. I'll be there for back up if you want. You're my partner until one of us drops dead."

"Thanks," she whispered.

"But, that six-figures though…" he said, sucking his teeth.

"Well, it was almost a touching moment…. nice job," Kim moaned.

"I'm playin with you," he laughed, "forreal talk to him, if you want out, get out, you know we gotchu, in or out, we're your family."

"Yeah, I know," Kim said opening the car door. "I'll see you later."

"Aye don't stay out too late, I heard there's assassins in this city," he teased.

"Right," she rolled her eyes slamming the door shut.

"Be safe," he told her.

34

"Always," she replied.

He exited the parking spot and sped off.

Kim always appreciated him. As annoying as he could be at times he was always on her side, always looking out for her. If there was anything she knew she would miss from The Pool if she left, it would be the company of the people she came to know while a part of it.

Suddenly a painful migraine came over her head that caused her to wince, but she quickly shook it off. She turned around and began heading back to her car but caught a figure waving at her out the corner of her eye. She glanced over and saw Helena smiling, sitting on the base of the statue where Kim had waited for her earlier. Kim stomped over to her.

"Hey beautiful, what's up?" Helena asked with a smile.

"Where have you been?" Kim demanded.

"Sitting here waiting for you to finish talking to your assassin friend."

It rattled Kim a bit that she addressed Pedro as such but she chose to ignore it.

"No, you told me to meet you here at seven?" Kim reminded her.

"I said seven-ish," Helena corrected her.

"OK.... either way it's going on eight, you're late."

"I mean I guess.... technically..."

Kim was far past annoyed, she closed her eyes and tried to calm herself down.

"Forget it. I wanted to talk, try to figure some things out but it's not even worth it, I'm going home."

"What?" she said standing up, "Kim, I just got here."

"Yeah and I'm leaving. I've been waiting on you for long enough, I'm tired, I need to go, and really I'm just not up for this anymore."

"OK OK, let's try again next weekend?"

Kim shook her head, "No."

"C'mon don't be silly, I promise I'll be on time next time."

She reached into her back pocket and pulled out a small piece of scratch paper and a pen. She scribbled something down on it and handed it to her.

"Here, take my number."

Kim rolled her eyes as she took the paper and jammed it into her pocket.

"Text or call me anytime," Helena smiled.

Kim completely over the moment was about to turn and walk away before she noticed something odd. She looked her over for a second and noticed Helena was wearing the exact same clothes she had on yesterday at the grocery store.

"Have you been home since last night?" Kim asked her.

Helena appeared caught off guard by the question.

"Home? Nope," she answered smiling.

Kim stared at her puzzled.

"Say hey to Cindy for me," she grinned.

"Yeah.... I'm not gonna do that," Kim said as she turned away and headed for her car.

She heard Helena giggle a little behind her

back.

"Bye Kim!" she shouted.

Kim kept walking without a word until she reached her car. She then looked back and saw Helena sitting at the base of the statue smiling, swinging her feet, watching cars maneuver in and out of spots. As she got in her car she kept her eyes on the girl. Something about her was oddly intriguing yet still, the way she carried herself made Kim so uncomfortable. She seemed too innocent for her own good, especially knowing the things she knew. It was horribly unsettling but she had to leave thoughts of her alone for now, she had to switch back to parent mode.

Chapter 3

Offset

"Ten, twenty, thirty, forty grand," Terrance counted out loud.

He pushed four stacks of bills bound together by rubber bands across the desk to Kim. She stared at the money unmoved at first. She eyed Terrance for a second and then shifted her gaze back down towards the money. He gave her a look as if asking her what she was waiting for.

"Problem? You wanna count it yourself, make sure I ain't cheat you?" he asked.

She sighed and swept the money off the table into a backpack sitting on the floor next to her.

"You good?" he asked.

"Yeah," Kim whispered, standing from her chair.

"Nah, sit down," he said.

She dropped back down into her seat refusing to look up.

"Kim, I know when something's bothering you, but you gotta talk to me. I'm not a mind reader and I'm not gonna pretend to be."

"It's nothing really..."

He didn't believe her; it was obvious she was disturbed. Kim had always been quiet, but she was currently just mute, she wasn't herself and he could tell. However, he refused to press her if she wasn't ready to talk about it.

"Alright, well on another note, Pedro told me you two talked last night?"

"I mean, I saw him yeah, we talked a little."

"So he told you about the contract we got?"

"Yeah, but listen…"

Kim shifted in her chair before taking a deep breath.

"I don't know if I still wanna…"

"Kim…. really? This again?" he interrupted.

"Why don't you get it?" she asked.

"Maybe cause you won't explain it, you just say you don't want to."

"And why's that not enough?"

He grew quiet. He leaned back in his chair and placed a hand over his chin.

"Kim, I'm not gonna make you stay, I can't, I know your folks would want you to be happy above all else. Let me remind you though, it's a possible upwards of six-figures for this one."

He slid a few papers across the desk towards Kim.

"Now, not that you need it, but it'd be nice right?"

She didn't even bother looking at the papers; she had seen money in massive amounts for six years now, so the payout meant nothing to her.

"Think about it," he whispered.

Kim stood up, threw her backpack over her shoulder, and left without another word.

~

Kim arrived home and quietly snuck into the house. She had left early in the morning to collect her money from Terrance, careful not to wake Cindy. She dropped her backpack in the corner next to the coat rack and walked to the kitchen. The backpack held about eighty-thousand dollars in cash and she wasn't in the least bit concerned leaving it lying around. She had carried bags holding larger sums before.

She walked into the kitchen, picked up an apple, and bit into it. She took a step to her right, standing in front of her refrigerator. On it, bound by a magnet, was a polaroid photograph that was mostly destroyed. All that remained was half of the photo favoring the bottom left corner. On the right side of the photo there looked to be a man in a black zip up jacket and jeans, and on the left side a woman in a red sundress holding a small child. However, nothing above the man and woman's neck was visible as the upper portion and most of the right side of the photo had been burned off entirely

The photo was special to her. It was of her and her biological parents, or her and their torsos rather. She was always told she was found abandoned amongst the chaos of a gang raid on her neighborhood. This separated her from her parents when she was just an infant. The photo as it was had been tucked into a blanket wrapped tightly around her. The only other thing with her was the chain she wore with her name on it. It had been wrapped several times around her leg to keep it from sliding off.

She gently thumbed over the charm resting against her chest as she studied the photo. The items were all she had to remember her real parents by, and they weren't much, so she treasured both as prized possessions.

She took another bite from the apple and sighed. She then looked up and saw the framed photo of her foster parents she had rested on top of the refrigerator. They were both fair skinned with jet black hair. Her father's slicked back and her mother's hanging down well past her shoulders. They both smiled wide as they embraced, staring deep into each other's eyes; they couldn't have looked more in love. To her, they were the most beautiful couple in the world and somehow, she was fortunate enough to have been their daughter for a time.

She shook her head slightly looking back and forth between the two photos. She couldn't help but pity herself.

She then noticed the sound of the TV in the living room. She was surprised, not expecting Cindy to be up so early on a weekend.

"Hey kid," she poked her head around the corner and immediately froze.

The apple fell from her hands and her jaw

dropped as she caught view of a familiar wardrobe. A white top, ripped blue jean shorts, a black beanie, and red sneakers. She cursed under her breath. Helena sat kicked back on her couch watching TV with the remote in her hand.

"Hey…. adult?" Helena responded with a funny look.

Kim quickly tucked her chain, pulled her hair pick from her waist, and rushed at her. She snatched the remote from her hand, pushed her back into the couch and pointed her hair pick's blade at her face.

"How did you get in my house?!" she demanded.

"Whoa," Helena said with her hands up, "how bout a good morning Helena, nice to see you again? Didn't realize we were skipping right to the part where we start pulling weapons on…"

"Answer me!"

"You left the door open…" she said softly.

"Are you kidding me? My daughter is upstairs, you don't just walk in people's houses, how did you even find out where I live?"

"Wait? Are you actually mad right now?" she asked grinning.

Kim grabbed her by her arm and pulled her to the front door.

"Well this is about as warm of a welcome as I've ever had."

Kim pushed her outside and stared at her with fiery eyes.

"If you ever come near this house again, I will kill you."

She viciously slammed the door in the girl's face.

"Mom?!" Cindy called from upstairs.

Kim rushed up and burst into Cindy's room to see her lying in her bed.

"Are you OK?" Kim asked in a panic.

"Yeah? Who were you talking to down there, I heard you all the way up here?" she asked, stretching her arms up.

"Work.... they're trying to cut some of my hours and I was just frustrated..."

She lied, choosing not to alarm her of Helena's intrusion.

".... it sounded like you were yelling at someone and then you slammed the door on them?"

"No no, don't worry about it. Hey, have you been downstairs today?"

"No, I've been in bed."

"Did anyone come by?"

"No, was someone supposed to?"

"No, just checking."

"Wait, where'd you go this morning, I heard you leave."

"I just.... went for a drive..." Kim looked away as she spit out another lie.

".... OK I guess," Cindy said unsure.

Kim closed the door, preventing any eye contact between them. The exchange was awkward, the situation was even stranger though. How could Helena have just walked in she wondered? She tried to remember if she really had been so careless as to leave the door open. She then began to think even

43

deeper. She remembered she hadn't gone into the living room before leaving earlier that morning. She began wondering how long she had actually been in the house.

"I'll have breakfast ready in about twenty minutes..." she called from behind the door.

~

"Kim?!"

Kim's head shot up from her work desk. She looked around nervously finding only her co-worker William, a tall, very slim, dark skinned man. For the better part of five years that Kim knew him he was always very clean cut and well dressed.

He was one of the few people she actually spoke with at her office job. He owed Kim a favor and managed to land her the job of which she had no real experience or qualifications for.

"You OK?" he asked.

"Yeah," Kim sighed, "I didn't really get any sleep last night, just tired."

She rubbed her eyes before burying her face in her hands.

"No sleep? Why, what's goin on?" he asked.

The truth was the night before she stayed up making sure she had no unwanted visitors after Helena's intrusion that morning. She knew she would be better off not mentioning it though.

"Just had a busy weekend," she told him.

"Well you better wake up, the boss sees you drooling all over your keyboard you'll get chewed out," Max, another co-worker of Kim's warned her.

Max was Kim's other only work friend, relatively new to the office. He was extremely tall, towering over both Kim and William. His pale white face was freckled and his hair was always unkempt. Much to the opposite of William he was hardly ever dressed well.

"Wouldn't be the first time," she moaned.

Kim worked in a building that focused mainly on seeking out gift matching opportunities. Her job was to reach out to donors through email and inform them of matching gift programs within the companies they worked for.

A noble and respectable work most would agree, but as Kim told it to anyone who asked, all she did was send a million emails a day to a million people she didn't know asking for money. It really only served to annoy and stress her out more and more each day than anything else.

"Go get some coffee or something," William laughed, "before you pass out again."

"No," she twisted her face at him, "I can't stand coffee. Smells awful and tastes even worse. It's like liquid cigarettes."

"So you're just gonna sleep, get fired, and then be homeless," Max asked.

"Sounds about right," she mumbled, closing her eyes and laying her head back down.

"No you won't, we get paid the same so I know you need this job," William said.

He grabbed her arm and pulled her up dragging her to the break room.

Kim hated having to keep her assassin work secret. Having people believe she actually needed her job made them constantly worry for her, and she hated being worried about.

"Just one cup and you'll be good for the rest of the day."

"Will, I don't want any coffee, I just wanna go to sleep."

"Well you're at work Kim, you can't go to sleep right now."

He pressed a few buttons on the coffee maker and opened up one of the cabinets above. Kim leaned against the counter struggling to stay awake.

"Man," William sucked his teeth, "hold on, we're out of cups, I'mma grab some real quick from the storage room."

Kim looked around the room, shifting her gaze slowly. She saw the fake plants in each corner, the cheap chairs around the two glass top tables, and a window with a small view of the parking lot. She focused on the coffee maker for a while; looking at the buttons, listening to the sounds it was making, attempting to figure out what it was even doing. She had never used one before in her life, yet in the moment of being tired out of her mind, it became oddly intriguing to her.

Its power cord was wrapped all around the machine's body as it was much longer than the space it had on the counter. Kim, halfway out of consciousness, began to slowly untangle it. After messing with it for a few seconds she had somehow gotten her arm tangled within the cord.

"Havin trouble with that?" a voice behind her asked.

Startled, Kim jumped, cursing aloud as she pulled her arm away bringing the entire coffee maker down to the floor by the cord. It hit the ground with a loud crash and broke into several pieces. Kim brought her attention up from the destroyed appliance to see Helena sitting at one of the glass tables across from her. She had a look on her face that suggested she had been just as spooked as Kim had.

"Awww…. man, that's comin out your paycheck," she teased.

Kim said nothing; she was again surprised to even see her. She looked her up and down noticing she was again wearing the same thing she had worn the day they met at the store.

Four of Kim's co-workers including William and Max stuck their heads in the doorway reacting to the loud crash. Kim's face began to turn red. She could only imagine how silly she looked with her arm tangled in the cord as the coffee maker laid on the floor in pieces.

"OK I know you didn't want any but you didn't have to destroy…"

"No, I didn't, I mean I didn't mean to…. she scared me," Kim explained, cutting William off.

She bent over trying to pick up the pieces.

"Who scared you?" William asked.

"She di…" Kim stopped mid-sentence as she looked over and noticed Helena was gone.

She had vanished just as she had in the grocery store the night they met. Kim stood up straight and looked around the small room puzzled.

"What? she was right.... there," she whispered.

"Kim, you may need to go home," William said.

"No, she was just here."

"Who?"

"Helena?"

William looked at Max and the other two standing behind him. They all shrugged.

"There's no Helena in this building Kim, everyone's at their desk anyway."

"No, wait a minute," Kim pulled her arm free from the cord and pushed through the four of them standing in the doorway.

She looked out on the office floor but only saw her co-workers all staring back at her confused.

"Someone had to have seen her, long blonde hair, she was wearing a hat, had a tattoo of a rose on her shoulder?"

She was met with only more confused stares.

"Kim, I'll talk to the head of our division, go home, you need to get some sleep," William told her.

"What.... no, I'm not crazy. She was here, someone had to have seen her," Kim insisted.

"C'mon, I'll walk you out," he said, putting his arm around her.

"But..."

"C'mon, it's fine," he said, quieting her.

The eyes of everyone on the floor were on them as they made their way towards the exit. Kim was puzzled, wondering how the girl had managed to go unseen by everyone in the office but her.

~

William drove Kim's car to her house as
another co-worker tailed them there for William to
catch a ride back with. The ride to the house was
quiet. Kim was too embarrassed to speak. She felt
like she was losing her mind. She knew what she had
seen, she knew who she had seen, she knew she was
there.

William pulled into Kim's driveway and
parked. They both got out and met each other at the
front of the car.

"Thanks Will," she said, as she took the keys
from him.

"No problem, please get some rest and be back
tomorrow, the higher ups have been hinting at letting
some people go they feel aren't performing in their
positions and I'm worried they may be looking at you
taking so many sick days and everything you know."

"Yeah," Kim said, barely acknowledging him.

"I'll see you tomorrow."

She nodded.

He got in the car that trailed them and left Kim
standing in her driveway alone. She looked up at the
sky and sighed deeply. She put her hands flat on the
hood of her car resting all her weight on her arms.
Looking directly down she saw her reflection on the
car's glossy paint job. She hated what she saw, to her
the person was unrecognizable. She looked tired, sad,
beaten, defeated; she just looked like a mess.

"Hey? Kim?" a voice immediately picked her

head up.

She looked left and saw her neighbor, best friend, and foster sister Luanne, who everyone called LuLu.

She was about the same age as Kim, slightly shorter but far heavier and curvier. She had rosy cheeks and long black hair she usually always had tied up in a bun on the top of her head.

She was a southern bell, evident by her deep south accent, who had somehow ended up in a foster home on the west coast of the country. They met and cliqued immediately when Kim was sent back to the foster home after losing her foster parents. They remained close as they became adults and no matter how hard Kim pushed her away she remained loyal to her and their friendship. While at first she didn't understand it, Kim eventually found a deep appreciation for her and her loyalty over the years.

"Hey, you alright?" she asked, crossing her yard into Kim's driveway.

"Yeah," Kim said, shaking herself from her trance.

"You sure, what are you doin home so early?" she asked.

Kim tried to conjure up another lie on the spot but eventually decided there was no point.

"I was tired, couldn't stay awake and they sent me home."

"Did they fire you?" LuLu's eyes widened.

"No no, they just sent me home for the day."

"Well that's good. Why were you so tired though, what's going on?"

"Just a lot on my mind at the moment," she said clinching the bridge of her nose between her fingers, "just haven't been getting a lot of sleep."

"Do you wanna talk about it?" she asked.

Kim appreciated how she would always ask and never force her to talk. LuLu was there when needed but also knew when to give her space.

"There's nothing to really talk about, it's all in my head really. I just gotta get my mind right," she assured her.

"Alright well hey, since you're off so early, you wanna grab lunch? Monday's aren't too bad for me, I'm up to date on all my assignments and..."

"Not right now Lu. I'm sorry, I just really need a nap, maybe another time," Kim told her.

She loved LuLu like a sister, but she didn't feel she had any focus at the moment. She just needed time to herself.

"Alright, no problem, well I hope you get to feeling better. Call me if you need anything. Tell Cindy I said hey too," she smiled.

"I will," Kim forced a smile back.

LuLu walked back over to her house and through the door. Kim let out another deep exhale and shook her head before pushing off the car's hood and heading inside.

Once in the house she immediately went to the living room and checked that no one was there. Once she confirmed she was alone she went to the kitchen and decided to make herself some warm tea. She loved warm tea, always had, it always calmed her down, allowed her to think.

She put a pot of hot water on the stove and sat down at the kitchen table taking a moment to relax and collect her thoughts.

She got so relaxed that she eventually fell into a nap. Very rarely was she ever able to sneak naps into her daily routine. Having to keep all her priorities in check and as far apart from each other as possible at all times just didn't allow for much relaxation. It was refreshing and rejuvenating to finally get just a few moments of peace, time to just unwind.

However, as none of her moments of peace did, it didn't last long. The ringing of her doorbell instantly rattled her. Upon waking up she immediately heard the sound of her teapot screaming. She had an idea of who was on the other side and it made her furious to even think about. She tried to ignore it, but a second ring came shortly after the first. Annoyed, she stood, shut off the heat from under the teapot, and stomped over to the door ready to give an earful to her for making her look so foolish earlier. She jerked the door open ready to unleash a wrath of words upon her but was surprised not to see who she thought she would, but Pedro instead. He cowered back a bit seeing her face full of anger.

"Whoa, you OK?" he asked.

"Yeah, sorry, rough morning. What's up?" she asked leaning against the doorframe.

"Was riding by, saw you were home early, thought I'd stop by and speak."

"Hmmm…. you always ride by my house when I'm not home?"

Pedro rolled his eyes at her comment.

"Whatever, look I wanna talk to you about something, can I come in?"

"Actually, I was just about to get a nap, I'm really not feelin well at the moment and I just need some rest, can it wait?"

"Look just hear me out. I know you said you're thinkin about walkin but Kim…. that check is lookin…"

"You know I don't care about money."

"Kim, it's one night…"

"It's probably more like one hour but that doesn't change my mind, the more I continue to do it the harder it becomes to step away from it, and I don't wanna be in this for the rest of my life."

"Think about it…" he pleaded.

"I don't know why y'all keep telling me to think about it, thinking is how I've come to the conclusion I don't wanna do this anymore, can't you take it alone?"

"C'mon you know Big Dog's not lettin me take nothin alone," he moped.

Kim slightly shook her head in silence, clenching her nose.

"Look I'm sorry Pedro, I don't know what you want me to say but…"

"We came from literally nothing Kim, you know that, I'm just trying to take care of myself and my family you know?"

He played this card often and Kim fell sucker to it every time.

"Yeah, I get it…. look I'll think about it," she

sighed, regretting it almost immediately.

"Thank you," he said, pressing his hands together.

"Yeah..." she sighed under her breath.

She began to close the door, tired of talking.

"Wait, hold on, you know you're family too, aside from all that, what's goin on, you look like you got something on your mind."

"Just tired...."

"Kim.... c'mon."

She hated letting people in her mind but she figured if she could tell anyone Pedro would be the easiest, plus she knew he wouldn't leave until she did.

"OK look, something kinda weird has been happening, someone keeps showing up, like, I might be being stalked."

"By who?"

"Some teenage girl..."

".... a teenage girl?" he slowly repeated.

She read the look on his face and immediately regretted saying anything.

"You know what, never mind, I didn't realize how stupid that sounded until it came out my mouth. I'm probably just messed up cause I'm sleep deprived."

"Kim..."

"No no, really don't worry about it, look I really gotta go. I can barely keep my eyes open right now, I'm sorry."

"Kim?"

She closed the door on him before he could say anything. She felt bad but relieved. She pressed her back against the door, closed her eyes, and took a deep breath. She stood there motionless for a few minutes wishing time would just freeze and give her a chance to just exist. Time without having to worry about things happening or people wanting to talk, but life just wasn't that kind to her. A sudden knock at the door broke her few minutes of peace and quiet just as the doorbell had before. Pedro prying again she assumed. She knew he was just trying to help and she loved him for it but she needed to be alone.

"Pedro please…" she jerked the door open and immediately stopped.

Helena stood at her doorstep carrying a large box, a coffee maker box.

"Sorry K, you just missed him, but I gotchu something though," she said, smiling holding the box out to her.

Kim looked past her, scanning around the neighborhood, then back at her.

"Uhhh…. it's kinda heavy so…" she handed the box over to Kim and then pulled a receipt out her pocket. She laid it on top of the box and proceeded to walk right past her into the house.

"You know, I didn't get to tell you the other day cause, well, you pointed a knife at my face and then threw me out, but you got a nice place here," she said as she eyed all around.

Kim still stood at the door holding the box as Helena wandered around inside. Kim felt like she was dreaming, she couldn't believe the girl. She seemed to have no conscience, no fear. Her head began pounding. She'd had enough of her.

She slammed the door closed with her foot, dropped the box to the ground and turned around.

"Hey!" she called out to her.

Helena poked her head from around the corner into the main hallway.

"Hey?" she responded lightly.

"Sit down, now!" Kim said harshly, pointing towards the kitchen.

Like a child caught misbehaving, Helena drug herself over to the kitchen table and sat down. Kim circled the table with her hand on the top of her head thinking for a few seconds. She eventually sat down directly across from her. She glared across the table at her as she smiled back arrogantly.

"So, I like tea too, if you wanna..."

"Shut up," Kim said, cutting her off.

"My my, where are your manners Kimberly?" she teased.

"Who are you?" Kim asked her.

"K, we've been over this..." she laughed.

"Actually, we haven't, you just kinda showed up and swore we knew each other."

"Cause we do, we go way back."

"Way back where? The first time I ever saw you was at the grocery store Friday night."

"You mean where you ran me over with your cart and almost stabbed me," she laughed.

"You're like at least five years younger than me, there's no way I am who you think I am, you must have me confused with someone else and I'd appreciate it if you stopped following me."

Helena bit her lip taking a moment to think.

"Nah," she shook her head, "sorry, can't do that Kim."

Kim batted her eyes in disbelief.

"I'm sorry, you must've misunderstood. I'm not asking you, I'm telling you to stay away from me, my house, and my daughter. Didn't I tell you last time you came here that if I saw you again I'd kill you?"

"And yet here I am still kickin," she smiled resting her chin in her hands.

"Where are your parents? Do they know you're stalking me? Where do you live? How did you find out where I live? And why have you been wearing the same clothes for four days?"

"So, should I just pick one of those questions or are we going through all of them?" she asked.

"I am so close to murdering you right here on this table. I'm not playing games with you kid, talk!" she commanded, slamming her hands on the table.

Helena crossed her arms, rolled her eyes, and sighed deeply.

"Well…. to answer one of those…"

She was suddenly interrupted by Kim's cell phone buzzing in her pocket. Helena shot a smirk at Kim but she refused to budge.

"Could be important," Helena grinned, egging her on to answer it.

Kim blew air through her teeth and stood up pressing forcefully on the table.

"Don't move," she told her.

Helena leaned back in the chair with her hands behind her head.

"Poor me a glass of tea while you're up babe?" she asked.

Kim ignored her as she answered the phone but kept her eyes on her to ensure she couldn't disappear again.

"Hello? Yes? What? OK OK, I'll be there shortly, thank you," Kim said, shaking her head.

She hung up the phone and then swore under her breath.

"Sounds like I was right, what's goin on?" Helena asked.

"My daughter got in a fight at school, I gotta go pick her up."

"What?! Little Cindy's scrappin now? K, she may be on her way to being just like you, first she gives a few black eyes, then next thing you know she's out on contract..."

Kim looked at Helena so furiously she hushed herself. Kim moved closer until she was right in her face. Helena held a surprised expression but a slight smile still peeked through.

"Don't you ever say that about her, she will not make the same mistakes I have," Kim told her.

She was adamant about this, she promised herself she wouldn't allow Cindy to fall into the life she was currently living, she wanted her to do something better, safer, less sinful.

"My bad?" Helena said, putting her hands up.

"Get out of my house," Kim growled.

"What about your questions?"

"My daughter is more important than anything I have to say to you, plus I'm pretty sure you'll show up again somewhere I don't want you to."

"True, very true," she agreed.

Kim watched as Helena made her way out the door smiling. She grabbed her keys and stepped out the house behind her.

~

Kim arrived in the main office of Cindy's school where she saw Cindy sitting in a chair with her head leaning against the wall. She sat right next to her much to Cindy's dismay.

"Hey kid, you OK? You're not hurt are you?" she asked.

"No, I hit her. She didn't touch me," she mumbled.

"You wanna tell me what happened?"

She exhaled heavy and rolled her eyes. It was obvious she didn't.

"There's this kid who sits alone every day at lunch and just cries. He never eats or talks to anyone. He just sits there and cries and everyone makes fun of him. I figured he was crying because he couldn't afford lunch and I was right. So for the past few days I've been giving him mine and today a few girls decided to make fun of both him and me. They were just getting on my nerves, one of them got in my face, and I hit her."

Kim closed her eyes, shook her head, and smiled a little to herself.

"It's not funny Mom," Cindy cried.

"You're right it's not." she said, "I'm laughing

because I came up here thinking I had a bad kid, but you did the right thing. I'm proud of you."

"You're proud? I'm probably getting suspended."

"Yeah, but you know what, sometimes doing the right thing'll get you in trouble, but that doesn't make what you did wrong. Your heart was in the right place; you helped that kid and stood up for him and yourself. I can't be mad at you for that."

"So, I'm not in trouble?" she asked, turning towards her.

"With me, no, but I can't say what your school's gonna think."

She turned back away from her and rested her head back on the wall. They sat there for a moment in silence. Kim looking straight ahead and Cindy with her eyes closed with her head rested against the wall.

"Where'd you hit her?" Kim asked.

"What?" Cindy asked.

"You get her in the mouth?" Kim asked.

"Oh my god..." Cindy breathed.

"Just askin," Kim smiled, quietly laughing.

A very tall man in a leisure suit walked into where they were sitting and over towards them. He had salt and pepper hair and a dead expression on his face.

"Hello, are you Cindy's mother?" he asked.

"Yes, Kim," she responded, standing and shaking his hand.

"Thank you for coming."

"Of course,"

"Follow me back to my office and we can

talk."

The three of them made their way back to a cramped office space. Kim and Cindy sat down around a desk pushed against the wall of the office.

"OK..." he began.

"Now, sir, please, Cindy just told me what happened and I really feel like you should listen too. It may give you a different way of looking at things. She's a good kid, I'm sure you can gather that from this being the first time you've ever had any trouble out of her."

"I hear you and I understand where you're coming from and I do know the details surrounding the situation. Cindy already shared them with me. However, Cindy threw the first and only punch and so just like with any other situation we must stick by our zero tolerance policy when it comes to violence."

"I understand," Kim said quietly.

"We have a minimum five day suspension for fighting which..."

"Whoa five days, don't you think that's a little harsh?" Kim interrupted.

"Ma'am she broke a girl's nose?" he added.

Kim turned to Cindy and discreetly smiled.

"You broke her nose?" she whispered, nudging her.

Cindy looked at her in shock and then at the man behind the desk, who was looking at Kim even more surprised. Kim looked up at him embarrassed.

"I'm.... I'm so sorry. But really five days is kinda harsh don't you think? I mean her heart was in the right place."

"That may be true but we cannot budge on a zero tolerance policy."

"I understand, is this effective immediately?" Kim asked.

"Yes, she'll be allowed back Tuesday of next week," he said.

"Alright, thank you," she said standing up.

"If you could just sign her out at the front desk before you leave."

"Yes sir," she said, shaking the man's hand, "you have a great day."

The two made their way back to the main office lobby where they stood alone.

"Well, that went well," Cindy said.

"Sorry Cin, I tried."

"Yeah, the part where you laughed about the girl's broken nose really helped."

"Hey look, I don't know a parent that's OK with their child not knowing how to defend themselves. Don't worry about it though, you're a good student, you've always been. A week away won't put you behind too much. You did the right thing. That's what's important."

"If you say so." she shrugged, "I'll be outside."

Kim stood at the front desk for a moment waiting for someone to show up so she could sign Cindy out for the day.

"Awww…. she's a good kid Kim, really good, you're doing a great job with her."

Kim turned around to the row of chairs she and Cindy had been sitting in earlier to see Helena now sitting in one. Kim swore under her breath.

"Will you go away?" she scoffed.

"I told you I can't do that," she stood up and walked up to the counter standing beside Kim, "but seriously it warms the heart knowing she was sticking up for that kid."

"How did you even hear that? Where were you listening from?"

She hoisted herself up and sat on the counter.

"I hear everything Kim."

"That's cause you're stalking me," she told her.

"Stalking?" she threw her hands out and hit a candy dish resting on the counter.

It wobbled a bit before tipping off the counter and crashing to the floor shattering into pieces.

The loud noise gave Kim a sharp spike of pressure in her head.

"Oops," Helena said looking down at the shattered dish.

"Really?" Kim scolded her.

She looked around and noticed they were all alone. She stepped behind the secretary's desk and grabbed the sign out sheet. She quickly signed her name and Cindy's and retreated from the office. Helena hopped down from the counter and poked her head out the door.

"Hey, you're not gonna help me clean this up?" she asked.

"I didn't do it!" she called over her shoulder.

~

The ride home was quiet. Neither Kim nor Cindy said anything. Cindy stared out the window the entire ride while Kim kept her head straight forward as she drove. When they finally pulled up to the house Kim stopped Cindy before she got out.

"Hey, what made you give that boy your food?" she asked.

"I don't know," she shrugged.

"You like him?"

"Stop, he was crying. I just thought he might be hungry, that's it."

Kim smiled.

"Alright," she took the keys out of the car and handed them to her, "you can go inside. I'm gonna walk next door and ask your Aunt Lu to come check on you while you're here by yourself this week."

"Alright," she said, stepping out of the car.

As Cindy walked to the door Kim watched her and smiled. She was proud of her and proud of herself. She always doubted how good of a parent she actually was but there were times when Cindy did things that let her know she was at least doing a halfway decent job. Those times were the things that kept Kim going on her toughest days.

Once Cindy was inside, Kim's smile faded as she turned around and stared into her backseat. Helena stared back at her with a smile.

"What's up? You two were pretty quiet on the way back, you good?" she asked.

Kim gave her nothing but a blank stare.

"You look mad."

Kim turned back around in her seat, took a

deep breath, and closed her eyes before speaking.

"I've been trained for multiple years on how to read people from their tone of voice, mannerisms, and actions. I don't know who you are or where you came from but I know you pose no real threat to me or anyone else. I can sense that much from you and that's the only reason you're still alive. But past that, I can't get a read on you, and that's making me incredibly uncomfortable. So, I'm gonna ask you again, and I want an answer, no games. I want the truth. Who are you?"

Just as she had earlier in the day, Helena seemed reluctant to give an answer to her question. She lifted up her chin for a minute switching between several facial expressions as she searched for the right words. Once she found them, she spoke them with confidence.

"I'm an offset, *your* offset," she said with a nod and smile.

Kim opened her eyes and turned back around to face her.

"An offset?" she repeated.

"Yep."

"That's it, that's your answer, an offset?"

"You asked for the truth right? I'm your offset. I'm here to help you."

"Please, leave me alone, I don't need your help with anything. If I ever do, I'll call you," she said softly.

"Call me?" Helena repeated puzzled.

"Yes, I still have your number from Saturday. I will call you if I need you, OK?" Kim said trying not to explode on her.

A confused look remained on Helena's face for a few seconds before she finally broke into another smile.

"Awww…. Kim," she laughed, "I don't even have a phone, I drew a picture of a bunny on that piece of paper."

Kim got out of her car and opened the door to the back seat where Helena was sitting. She bent down so she could see her face.

"Get out of my car, and leave me alone," she said in the deadest of tones.

Helena laughed.

"Love you Kim," she said, as she scooted out of the backseat.

She began walking down the sidewalk whistling a tune. Kim could only watch both amazed and confused as she footed down the sidewalk. She winced as another migraine suddenly hit her and quickly passed.

Chapter 4

Joey

Kim yawned as she walked downstairs and into the kitchen. She was less than thrilled about the questions and stares she knew she would be getting at work after what had happened the day before.

As she entered the kitchen she scoffed at a red glass of tea left out on the table. She shook her head as she picked it up, poured what was left down the drain, and placed the glass in the sink to be washed later.

As she turned to step away she paused and looked back at the glass. She suddenly remembered Helena's words from the day before.

So, I like tea too, if you wanna...

She quickly raced back upstairs and down the hall to Cindy's room. She knocked twice before opening the door. Cindy was barely awake as she rolled over with her eyes squinted.

"Morning sweetheart, hey, did you make some tea last night?" she asked.

"No..." she said, arching her back stretching,

"why?"

"Ummm.... there was a glass left out on the table."

"The red one?"

"Yeah."

"That was yours," she moaned.

"I didn't make tea last night," she told her.

"Yeah you did, I saw you. You made it and then sat at the table staring at nothing while you drank it last night," she explained.

Kim tilted her head sideways at her.

"Are you sure?" she asked, now doubting her own thoughts.

She was sure she hadn't had tea, but Cindy wouldn't have a reason to say she saw her if she hadn't.

"I literally saw you drinking out of it."

"O-OK, maybe it was me," she said trying to jog her own memory.

"Are you OK?" Cindy asked.

"Yeah, I'm fine, I just.... have you seen anyone around the house lately?" she asked.

"What do you mean?" Cindy asked, slowly sitting up.

Kim feared alarming her. She already had reason to believe she was going insane and now not being able to remember the simplest of tasks like making tea only added more fuel to the thought. She chose to just leave it alone.

"Never mind, Aunt Lu's gonna check on you in between her classes, maybe call you a few times to make sure you're alright. Don't open the door for anyone else, OK?"

Kim's tone changed as she said this, it was more direct, harder.

"Is someone else coming?"

"No, just be careful, OK?"

".... Alright." Cindy shrugged.

Kim closed the door feeling both upset with herself and a bit embarrassed. She was acting suspicious and Cindy was too smart not to notice. She knew she needed to calm down and choose her words more carefully around her. She couldn't afford for her to start asking questions.

~

Kim stood at the window in the break room at work. She scanned the parking lot watching every inch of it. Nothing seemed to be out of order. There was nothing to see but a bird occasionally landing on a powerline or a car pulling either in or out of the lot. Nothing out of the ordinary, which for once bothered her.

"Kim..."

She jerked forward as a hand was placed on her shoulder. She turned around to see William.

"You scared me, " she sighed, turning back towards the window.

"Scared you? You scared me, what are you so jumpy for?" he asked.

"I'm not. You just spooked me."

He leaned over her shoulder a bit to get a view out the window himself.

"What are you looking at?" he asked.

"Nothing," she said disappointed, "nothing at all."

"Alright, well you should probably get back to your desk, boss has been noticing your absences here and there."

Kim rolled her eyes and sucked her teeth at his warning.

"Why's he always on me?"

"Uhhh.... maybe because you're either not at your desk, showing up late, or not showing up at all?"

She turned around and stared at him cutting her eyes a bit.

"Whose side are you on?"

"C'mon," he laughed, "you know I'm just trying to make sure your lights stay on."

"If you only knew how hard I'm trying," Kim said shaking her head.
The sarcasm in her tone missed him by a mile. Kim's cell phone quickly vibrated in her pocket. She pulled it out and blew air from her nose in a light frustration.

"What's up?" William asked, turning to make a cup of coffee.

"Cindy just texted me, we're almost out of tea. I just bought a whole box Friday."

"How do y'all drink that stuff?" he laughed.

"The same way y'all drink that dirt water," she fired back pointing at the coffee maker, "which, by the way, does it work? Cause if not, I'm taking it and getting my money back."

"It's fine, thanks for getting a new one by the

way. It'd have been rough in here this morning for a lot of people without it."

"I bet," Kim said, facing back towards the window.

"How is Cindy anyway?" he asked.

"Well, she broke a girl's nose yesterday," she mumbled over her shoulder.

"What?!" he asked, turning around.

"No, it's OK, she was doing the right thing."

"Uhhh..."

"It's complicated, don't worry about it she's fine." she said, waving off the topic, "Hey, you ever feel like you're being watched, or followed even?"

"You mean like you're doing to someone or something outside right now?" he teased.

"Hey," Max called from the doorway, "boss is on the floor looking over people's shoulders, y'all better hurry up."

"Ugh…. c'mon Kim, let's go," William urged her, grabbing his coffee and some napkins.

She didn't budge, remaining still, standing at the window, investigating everything in her line of sight.

"Kim?" he called again for her at the door.

"Coming," she whispered, tearing her focus from the window.

~

"A movie huh? No thanks, work kinda sucked today, my boss was on me all day I just really wanna relax. You two enjoy though," Kim said, holding her phone up to her cheek.

Kim pulled a box of tea down from a shelf.

"I'm at the store. Cindy and me have been running through this tea pretty fast I guess. She asked me to pick up some more on my way home."

LuLu had called to tell her she was going to take Cindy to the movies.

"Yeah, I'll be home when you guys get back. Have fun. I'll see you soon. Thanks Lu. Bye."

Kim grabbed another box of tea hoping two would last a little longer than one had. She also tried to shake the thought of someone else besides them being the reason the box seemed to disappear so quickly.

The day had been quiet, too quiet she realized. As she made her way up to the register, she panned her eyes from left to right. She made eye contact with no one but made sure to take a good profile of her surrounding area and everyone within it.

As she passed by one of the aisles a blur of red entered her peripheral that immediately made her stop. She bumped into it slightly before focusing fully on it. It was a person, a man about her same height, wearing a solid red hoodie.

"Oh! I'm so sorry, excuse me," she said flashing a fake smile.

"Oh, you're fine," he said, stepping backwards, removing himself from her path.

Kim was ready to pass him before she noticed him turn back in her direction.

".... Kim?" he asked.

She turned and looked the man in his face. She

saw his lightly freckled face, his messy hair sticking out from underneath a baseball cap turned backwards, and his slender frame. She immediately recognized him.

".... Joey?" Kim asked.

"Yeah," he smiled.

Joey was like Kim's younger brother. Like Kim, he was also born and raised in Joy City. They both attended the same schools growing up and while they weren't very close initially were always at least aware of each other. Back when she was in high school, Kim made friends with just about everyone she crossed paths with. Back then she was a very cheerful, optimistic, fun loving girl, someone everyone wanted to be around. Joey was no exception.

Though it wasn't until Kim lost her parents at fifteen and was sent back to the foster home did they become closer. Just a few months prior to this happening, Joey's parents had been killed. She wasn't entirely sure what happened but she heard it was a random act of gang violence, something not uncommon in Joy City. This sent him to the same foster home Kim spent her earliest years in and where she would shortly be sent back to, much to her dismay.

Being both around the same age and at the time, going through very similar circumstances, they could relate to each other and naturally became closer. However, as they both grew up and things changed, they lost touch over the years. None the less, being from the same foster home, they considered each other family.

"Hey, how are you?" Kim smiled.

She was happy to see he was OK. Losing his parents to murder, having gone through the same thing herself, she always felt for him and wondered about his wellbeing. She could attest it was tough to keep a straight path after experiencing such tragedy so young.

"Makin it," he said, cocking his head to the side, "How bout you?"

"Same really, taking it day by day," she responded.

"You still live here?"

"Unfortunately."

"Really? Back in school everyone figured you were on your way to taking over the world, thought you'd be on to somewhere big by the time you hit twenty."

In school Kim's friends would always poke at her calling her the golden child, as everything about her and her life did seem golden then. She was beautiful, charismatic, smart, and seemed on track to be the first person to ever come out of Joy City and matter to the rest of the world.

"Don't remind me," she scoffed, "I'm twenty-six, still living in this place, trying to find my way out. C'mon, walk with me. Let me get this stuff rung up."

They began a slow walk towards the front of the store.

"Well, aside from your addiction with this tea, what else is new?" he laughed, grabbing one of the boxes from her hands.

"Hey, it's great, me and Cindy run through boxes of this stuff like it's nothin," she smiled, snatching the box back from him.

"Cindy?" he asked.

"My daughter?" she said.

"You have a daughter?" he asked with wide eyes.

This was evidence of how long it had been since she and Joey had actually spoken. She had adopted Cindy five years prior and he didn't even know who she was.

"Yep, a full fifteen year old," she told him.

"Fifteen?!"

"Relax," she laughed, "she's adopted, we've been like best friends for some years now. Met her at Little Angels."

Little Angels was the proper name of the foster home Kim and her foster brothers and sisters grew up in. They all eventually began just calling it The Home.

"Oh yeah? That's awesome."

"You still live around here?" she asked.

She noticed he seemed reluctant to answer at first.

"Uhhh.... I guess."

"You guess? What's that mean? You do or you don't."

"I mean I don't really live anywhere, just kinda bounce around from friend to friend's house until they get tired of looking at me."

"What?" Kim asked, halting their walk.

"I mean I'm fine.... I just move around a lot is all," he told her.

Kim began to side eye him with a look of doubt. He couldn't lie to her; she was too good at reading people.

"Joey.... are you homeless?"

He refused to answer, immediately turning in the opposite direction, but she knew.

"Joey," she said, stepping closer to him, "you can't live on Joy City's streets. Trust me I know, I did it. You need to find somewhere to stay, permanently."

The big sister in her was coming out, she couldn't stand to think someone she considered her brother was in such a tough spot.

"Where?" he asked, "I don't have the money to afford the worst apartment in town."

"Go back to The Home then Joey," she suggested.

"I can't, there's no room for a twenty-five year old with all those kids in there."

Kim always thought of the foster home they grew up in as a safe haven because for her, for the longest, it was. Whenever she got tired of staying at Terrance's or being on the streets she could always come back and she would be welcomed back with open arms, even if she was being drug back forcefully. However, that was when she was still a teenager. It didn't occur to her that they had gotten several years older now. The head of the foster home was like a mother to them both. She loved them dearly, even now years after they had left. But at some point, she would have to deny them beds to ensure younger kids who had less options than they did as adults a safe place to lay their heads at night.

Kim twisted her face in disapproval. Joey bit his lip as he stared down at his feet saying nothing.

"C'mon let me pay for these," she whispered.

Kim paid for the tea and they made their way outside together to Kim's car. Neither of them spoke a word. Kim opened the doors to the back seat and threw the two boxes inside. She closed the door and turned to Joey standing behind her.

"So where are you going?" she asked him.

He shrugged, much to Kim's displeasure.

"Joey, really?" she said, rolling her eyes.

Her tone reflected that of a mother upset at her child. She was almost angry at him for seeming so fine with having no place to stay.

"I-I don't know..." he shrugged again, holding his hands out.

"Do you have any money?" she asked.

He shook his head no.

"So what were you doing in there?" she asked, pointing back towards the store.

He again refused to answer. He instead just sighed and stared at the ground.

"Were you gonna steal something Joey?"

"No..." he said, avoiding eye contact.

"Joey?" she grabbed the side of his face with one hand and turned it forcing him to look at her, "you can't lie to me."

She took his silence as a confession.

"Joey, why didn't you say something?" the

aggression in her tone picking up, "All you had to do was ask. I'd have bought you anything in there you needed."

"Kim, I'm fine," he assured her.

"Joey, you're..."

"Fine, I'm fine Kim," he said, finishing her sentence.

She took a deep breath and scratched her head as she released it, mumbling quietly to herself.

"Alright, get in," she said, motioning towards the passenger side of her car.

"What?"

"If you're not gonna let me buy you anything you're at least gonna let me make you something to eat."

"Kim, I promise I'm OK."

"I'm not asking, get in," she said sternly.

Joey simply submitted remembering how tough of a person she was to argue with. He got inside and they were off to her house.

~

"I really only stayed in contact with Blake and Lu after I left The Home for good. Blake because, well, you know, he wouldn't stop calling to check on me every day, and Lu lives right next door," Kim explained.

"LuLu lives next door?" Joey asked, stuffing a fork full of lasagna in his mouth.

"Yep, she's actually out at a movie right now with Cindy."

"Wow…. hmph…. I haven't seen Blake in forever, I talked to him on the phone a while ago but…. hey, you ever stop by The Home and visit?"

"Not as much as I should to be honest."

"Well if you went once in the past ten years you've done better than me."

He sounded disappointed in himself.

"Don't sweat it, you've had it rough. We all said we'd come back and visit and half of us haven't kept that promise."

Joey stood up and placed his paper plate in the trash.

"Yeah, just feel like I should do better you know?"

"And you can, but first you gotta get yourself situated. A place to stay. A job. Start taking steps towards turning your life around."

"I know I know," he said to her.

He turned away from her with his hands on his head as he paced in a small circle around the kitchen.

"If you need to, you can stay here until you get back on your feet."

"Thanks but no, I don't wanna be in your way."

"Joey, I'm barely here. Trust me you won't be in my way. If anything Cindy'll get tired of you before I do."

"I appreciate it and I'll keep it in mind but right now I don't think it's best," he told her.

Kim threw her hands up and shook her head in defeat, "Alright."

She stood up and threw her own plate in the trash.

"Thirsty?" she asked.

"Anything but that tea," he laughed.

"Oh trust, you weren't getting any of my tea anyway," she teased, "grab what you want out the fridge. I'll get you a glass."

Joey grabbed the handle on the refrigerator and paused. He was fixed on the destroyed photo on the front of it.

"Hey, Kim?" he slurred.

"Yeah?"

"What's this picture of?" he asked.

Kim walked over and stood next to him.

"Ahhh.... me and my parents. My biological parents. We got separated in those gang raids around the time Joy City got really bad."

"The 45s' raids?" he asked, turning to her.

"The 45s? The Colt 45s?" Kim asked.

"Yeah, that's the gang that raided the city about twenty or so years ago, they were burning neighborhoods to the ground back then."

Kim knew of the gang as they were notorious for terrorizing Joy City, still to the day. She also knew of them through The Pool. Sometimes The Pool paid them for intelligence of the streets when needed as they knew them better than they did. After being told how she was separated from her biological parents, she never really looked any further into it and so she wasn't aware the 45s were the ones responsible. It bothered her a bit to learn the gang she often worked with played a role in her separation from her family.

"Well yeah, we got separated somehow in all

that. I was of course way too young to remember what actually happened though, I've only really heard stories about it. As far back as I can remember I was bouncing from foster home to foster home until I landed at Little Angels. I really don't even remember them. The only things I have from them are the picture and this necklace."

Kim pulled her gold chain from her chest and held it out for Joey to see.

"Apparently when I was found, wherever or however that was, they found the picture on me all burned up and this tied around my leg. It being all I had to remember them by, I've worn it every day of my life since."

"So, if these are your birth parents in this picture, then who were you living with back in high school before you came to The Home?"

"My foster parents." Kim reached up to the top of her fridge and pulled down the framed photo. "They took me from The Home when I was about six. When they were killed, I just ended up coming right back."

She blew a layer of dust off the glass and handed the frame to him.

"I didn't know that." he whispered, staring at the photo intrigued, "So wait, *foster parents*? They didn't actually adopt you, just fostered you?"

"No they did adopt me but I don't know, foster parents just always rolled off the tongue better than adoptive parents to me, so that's what I always called them."

Kim noticed his eyes widened, he stopped

blinking, she believed he had even stopped breathing for a second as well. Then he cut his eyes and spoke slowly to her.

"Yeah, weren't they pretty rich? What'd they do for a living?" he asked, never removing his eyes from the picture.

"Dad invested his inheritance and flipped it into millions in his early twenties. He was a smart man."

A lie Kim had practiced for years.

"Inheritance huh?" he repeated.

His blank stare grew more and more intense as he studied the photo longer and longer.

"What happened to them?" he asked.

"Honestly, I'm not sure. I woke up one morning and there were a couple police officers downstairs with a few close friends of theirs, I came down and they told me they'd been murdered. With not much evidence to go on or any real leads to follow, the investigation, if you can even call it that, consisted of a pointless sweep of our house, a few questions asked that got them nowhere, and they left it cold."

"Sorry to hear that," he said with his eyes still glued to the photo.

Kim noticed how hard he was fixated on it. She started to believe the photos and stories of her parents and losing them might have been getting to him. She thought they might be bringing up bitter memories of his own parents. She reached and placed a hand on his shoulder and the other on the frame.

"You OK?" she asked.

He shook his head quickly as if breaking himself from a spell. He pushed the frame in her direction.

"Yeah."

Kim placed the frame back on top of her fridge. She felt bad thinking she may have accidentally struck a nerve.

"Joey, I'm sorry if..."

"I'm gonna head out," he said nervously adjusting his cap.

"What? Joey, where?" she asked.

"I don't know, I'll figure something out, don't worry about it," he said as he made for the door.

She rushed after him and grabbed his wrist.

"You're my brother, I'm always gonna worry about you," she said.

She could see in his eyes something was bothering him.

"I'm fine." he said, as he gently removed her hand from his wrist, "Thanks for the food. Tell Lu I said hey."

He started back towards the door.

"Wait," Kim said, quickly stepping back into the kitchen.

She pulled open a drawer and snatched out a pen and small notepad. She scribbled her cell phone number down on one sheet and tore it off the pad before handing it to him.

"If you ever need anything," she said.

He stuffed the piece of paper in his pocket and turned away from her without a word. With his head down, he opened the door and drug himself out to the sidewalk before turning right. Kim hung out the door contemplating following him but decided it was best not to press him. She understood one needing time alone.

She closed the door but moved the drapes hanging in front of the window aside and peeked out. She watched him until he was out of her line of sight. She placed a hand over her forehead which had begun throbbing. She sighed heavily, upset at herself.

She turned around and quickly pressed her back to the wall. She gasped and her heart nearly stopped at the sight of Helena standing in front of her.

"That was kinda odd?" she said.

"How long have you been in here?" Kim asked.

"I don't know?" she moved next to Kim and peeked out the window herself, "Hey, he was acting kinda weird don't you think?"

"Get out," she managed through a few heavy huffs of air.

"I mean he was cool and then all of a sudden he gets all quiet. And he was *super* into the pictures of your folks and then just leaves all in a hurry. Pretty suspect if you ask me."

"Get out," Kim repeated, breaking the words up more.

"I'm just sayin keep an eye on him K, he might be your brother but..."

Kim grabbed her arm and yanked Helena towards her.

"Get out!" she growled at her.

"You must be a great party host, your hospitality is just phenomenal," she teased.

Kim opened the door, pushed her outside, and slammed it shut before she could even turn back around. She locked the door and turned away.

"Love you babe!" Helena shouted from the other side of the door.

Kim ignored her as she climbed up the stairs massaging her head.

Chapter 5

Severed

"Cin, I'm gone!" Kim yelled, as she made her way down the stairs.

She was still groggy. She'd had another night without the sleep she so desperately needed. While Helena's unwanted presence remained on her mind, so did Joey. A full day had come and passed since she had run into him at the grocery store, and she hated knowing he wasn't doing well. She made up in her mind should she see him again, she wouldn't let him walk away. She would find a way to help him get himself together.

She was running a little later than usual, so she was moving quickly. She got to the front door, yanked it open and was stopped in her tracks.

"Hey girl, you in a rush?" a friendly face smiled.

Aaliyah stood at the door, another assassin of The Pool. She had a figure very similar to Kim's but was slightly taller. She had a beautiful shade of ebony skin, and very kinky curly hair. She had been in The Pool almost as long as Kim; she showed up about a half a year after her. She was often a foil to Kim in most instances. She dressed in bright colors, smiled often, and could find the fun in almost anything. When first introduced to her, Kim was surprised someone like her would ever want to be associated with something like The Pool, but figured it wasn't her place to question her motives.

She stood at the door with her fist held in mid-air. She was just about to knock as Kim opened the door.

"Yes actually," Kim said.

"But you can spare a few minutes for me right?" she smiled, batting her eyes.

"Aaliyah, I'm already late for work. It'll have to wait."

She attempted to move past her but Aaliyah cut her off stepping in front of her.

"How much time do you have?" she begged.

"Like thirty minutes."

"I only need two."

"And that leaves me with twenty-eight, which is not enough to get me fired, only written up and yelled at, sorry not worth it."

She tried to move past her again. Aaliyah again cut her off, extending her arms to the doorframe preventing Kim from passing.

"Kim, you're wasting your own time," she told her.

"*I'm* wasting my time?" Kim asked, pointing at herself.

"Just listen?" she begged again.

"Fine, hurry up."

"OK OK. Pedro told me you're not budging on this contract..."

"Oh my god no, I'm not having this discussion a third time," she rolled her eyes.

She ducked under Aaliyah's arms and shut the door behind her as she proceeded to walk towards her car.

"Kim?!" she cried.

"Bye Aaliyah!" she shouted over her shoulder.

"Just listen?!"

"I don't wanna talk about this," she exclaimed as she turned around walking backwards to her car, "why are y'all so unable to get off this? He asked me to think about it, and I have, I don't wanna do it."

She got in the car and started the engine. Aaliyah calmly walked over to her car with an haughty grin and stood at the window waiting. Kim buried her face in her hands realizing Aaliyah had parked her car directly behind hers. She rolled down her window glaring at her.

"Can you please move so I can go?" she gritted through her teeth.

"Oh, I got a please out of you? Are we being nice now? Are you willing to listen now?"

"Aaliyah," Kim pressed her hands together, "I have to go. I can lose my job if I'm late."

"Awww.... nice try Kim. You don't need that job, we both know that," she said.

Kim, aggravated, turned off the engine, stepped out of her car, and motioned Aaliyah towards the house.

Aaliyah smiled, "Love gettin my way."

~

Inside Kim and Aaliyah sat at the kitchen table and talked.

"It's not that we all just want to, as much as it just needs to be done," Aaliyah told her.

"Why do we *need* to kill anyone? Aren't we doin this literally just for the money? Half of these people don't deserve to die."

"Kim that's not our call and not our business, you know that, this ain't new to you."

Kim took a sip from a glass of tea.

"Where's this sudden compassion coming from anyway?" Aaliyah asked.

"There's no compassion. I don't care who it is or if they're innocent or not really. I just don't wanna be a part of it."

"You really steppin out huh?" she sighed.

"Every day feelin better and better about it," she said.

"Pedro needs you. Terrance won't let him take a contract alone."

"He won't let him go alone because he doesn't have to so long as I'm there. If he doesn't have a choice, I bet he will. I've trained him enough to know he'll be fine on his own."

"Alright," Aaliyah placed her hands on the table and pushed herself up from her chair, "it's your call."

Kim stood up with her. They walked to the

door together.

"So how's Cindy?" Aaliyah asked.

"Suspended."

Aaliyah flashed a surprised look at her.

"She broke a girl's nose," Kim said

Aaliyah's jaw dropped.

"It's OK, she was doing the right thing."

".... OK?" she said, with an eyebrow raised, "One more thing, just asking, I'm pretty sure I already know the answer but just to put it out there. We got a small contract tomorrow we could use an extra hand on deck if you're free?"

Kim leaned against the wall, crossed her arms and shot her a disgustingly fake smile.

"Oh Aaliyah, thank you for asking, I would love too," she said, in a horribly exaggerated tone.

"Right, didn't think so, just thought I'd ask," Aaliyah said.

She opened the door and stepped outside.

"Be safe," Kim said as she watched her leave.

"Always," she called over her shoulder.

Kim closed the door and fell back leaning against it. She closed her eyes and bit her lip as she thought for a moment. It was odd thinking about the conversations she had been a part of in the past six years of her life. What to her was a normal conversation would throw most people for a loop. Not to mention the things she had actually seen in the past six years, things that would make most sick to their stomach.

She stepped back into the kitchen to finish her tea but was drawn in by the ruined photo of her birth parents. She walked closer to look at herself, the only face viewable in the image. She was so young, so happy, so unaware of where she would end up, who she would become. She placed a finger on the singed edges of the photo and traced them. They were rough, jagged, harsh. She wondered had it been an omen that she was too young and blind to ever notice before?

~

"So wait, he's a god now?" Kim asked.

"Yes," Cindy responded.

"But he was a god before though, right?"

"Well yes, he's like a super god now."

Kim was in the living room with Cindy watching TV. She had no idea what they were looking at but Cindy was trying to explain it all to her, to barely any avail.

"So that's why he went from red to blue?" Kim asked.

"Yes."

"OK, so he's like the strongest person in the world now?"

"He's been that. He wants to be the strongest in all of the universes."

"*Universes?* As in plural?"

"Yes, there's twelve, but we only really care about the sixth."

Kim shook her head confused.

"OK, so who's the magic cat?" Kim asked.

"He's not magic, he's a god," Cindy corrected her.

"I thought the red blue guy was a god?"

"He is. They're both gods. There's multiple gods in all twelve universes."

Kim shook her head.

"Cin, this is kinda ridiculous."

"It's supposed to be."

Kim looked over at her. Her eyes were locked on the screen. Even in her confusion Kim couldn't help but smile. She didn't get to spend many moments with her but she always treasured the ones she did. With Cindy being suspended she decided staying home from work would be the perfect opportunity for them to spend a little time together.

The doorbell sounded, pulling Kim's attention as Cindy's remained on the TV.

"Probably your Aunt Lu coming to check on you, forgot to call her and tell her I was staying home today," Kim said rising from the couch.

"You're gonna miss it," Cindy whispered.

"It's OK, not like I've understood anything I've actually seen anyway," she said walking to the door.

Kim swung the door open much to LuLu's surprise.

"Hey, you been home all day?" she asked.

"Yes..." Kim said slowly.

"You had the day off?" she asked.

".... No," Kim answered, avoiding eye contact.

LuLu, believing Kim was struggling and needed her job to stay afloat, was always hard on her about taking days off and skipping work. She was afraid she would one day get fired and have to scramble to make ends meet.

"Kim?" she flashed her a disapproving frown.

"Sorry *Mom*," Kim moaned sarcastically, "I had a rough morning and decided to spend time with my daughter."

"Did you at least call in?"

"My co-workers got me, plus no one will even notice I'm gone," she assured her.

LuLu shook her head at her.

"Well, I was just coming to check on Cindy," she said.

"She's fine. Just watching TV. C'mon in."

The two of them made their way into the living room where Cindy was still laser focused on the TV.

"Hey sweetheart," LuLu greeted her.

"Hey Aunt Lu," she said, looking away for only a second.

"Sorry, she's a little preoccupied with this disaster of a show she's watching," Kim said.

"If you understood it you'd like it," Cindy remarked.

"Yeah yeah," Kim said walking back into the kitchen.

LuLu followed behind her.

"Want something to drink?" she asked.

"Anything but that tea you drink," she laughed.

"Why's everyone gotta talk about my tea?"

"It's disgusting Kim," she laughed again.

"Whatever," she handed her a bottle of water from the fridge, "what are you up to today?"

"School. Had a test this morning, pretty sure I bombed that. Got another one in about an hour. Loans piling up, stress, it's all bad right now," she said taking a sip.

"Just stay with it, it'll be worth it in the end," Kim told her.

"Hard to stay with it if I just can't afford it."

Kim hated that she couldn't help her. She had more than enough money to put LuLu through all the schooling she could possibly want, but if she found out she had that kind of money, she would have questions, questions she wasn't prepared to answer.

"I understand," she nodded.

"I'm just so tense right now, I feel like I'm about to explode," she said, shaking.

"Sounds like you need to get out, do something fun to take your mind off everything."

"Yeah...." she nodded, "Hey! Let's go out tomorrow night, me and you!"

"What?"

"Yeah, I know a place."

"No no, I'm good. Thanks though."

"Oh c'mon, you promised me another time Monday."

"I did not promise, I specifically remember saying maybe," Kim objected.

"Please Kim," LuLu grabbed her hand in her own, "you never go anywhere and it's been so long since we hung out, just this one time, please?

She started pouting, trying to guilt her into submission. Kim saw this and let out an annoyed sigh. She hated going out but also didn't want LuLu to feel like she was avoiding her.

"Where are you talking about going Lu?"

"It's that club that just opened down on..."

"A club? Oh no way, no, sorry, definitely not doing a club."

"Kim, it's not that type of club, it's just like a little fun place people go to hang out. Nothing crazy," LuLu assured her.

Kim was skeptical. She knew she was desperate and would say just about anything to get her to come along.

"We don't even have to stay for that long, there's gonna be a performance, we can get a few drinks, some food, and then head back home, please?"

Kim stared at LuLu with a look that told she didn't want to go. She wanted to decline, but she couldn't. Not with LuLu pouting at her.

"Alright alright," Kim groaned.

"Yes!" LuLu jumped in excitement.

"Whoa whoa, that's already too much energy, don't make me change my mind," Kim said, holding her still.

"Right right, sorry," she smiled.

"One hour, two tops," Kim told her.

"Got it, make sure you put on something cute."

"Yeah.... no, hoodie and sweatpants for me."

LuLu rolled her eyes smiling.

"You're no fun," she said.

"Finally, you're getting it."

LuLu sucked her teeth at her.

"Anyway, I'mma get back and finish out the day, take this test, and I'll call you tonight to figure out a time."

"I'm already regretting this," Kim sighed.

"Stop. It's gonna be great," she said making for the door.

"Doubt it," Kim mumbled.

"Bye Cindy!" LuLu shouted over her shoulder.

"Bye!" Cindy called back from the living room.

"Good luck with the test," Kim said as she headed through the door.

"Unfortunately luck won't do it, gonna need an act of God to make it through this one," she groaned.

"Bye Lu," Kim laughed under her breath as she closed the door behind her.

She would never tell her to her face but she was immensely appreciative of LuLu. Being known as the pretty, popular, rich girl, Kim never seemed to be short on friends growing up. Yet, after she lost her foster parents, and her life began to change, so did everyone around her. She became a loner, her disposition dipped, and as a result everyone distanced themselves from her. All her peers who seemed to love and adore her vanished, except LuLu.

Through the ups and downs she was always there encouraging her, attempting to be her friend, and always made sure Kim knew she cared about her. While it took awhile for her to realize it, Kim knew she was truly lucky to have her as a friend and sister.

She walked back to the living room and sat back down next to Cindy. She was still staring at the TV. Kim looked back at the screen herself and just shrugged in confusion.

"Cin, is that a man or woman?" she asked.

~

The next morning Kim set her alarm for an hour earlier than usual. Her sleep pattern had been thrown off as of recently. She knew if she didn't wake up earlier she would have a hard time rolling out of bed. She immediately jumped up to get ready for work.

Being up so early she walked downstairs to make herself some tea. When she got to the kitchen she flicked the light switch on and yawned. Her head went back, her eyes closed, and she stretched her arms up to the ceiling. When she dropped her head back down, she opened her eyes and there at her table with a glass of tea in her hand sat Helena. Smiling big as usual.

"Hey good lookin, you're up early today?" she grinned.

Kim just looked at her in awe.

"I literally don't have the strength to throw you out right now," she grumbled.

"So don't, let's talk instead." Helena patted the table inviting her to sit down, "Made you some tea."

Kim looked at the other glass of tea resting on the table across from where Helena sat. She hesitated for a moment. She wanted more than anything to throw her out again but just couldn't find the energy. She pulled the chair out from the table letting the legs drag across the floor. She stared menacingly at Helena as she sat down. She pulled the glass to her and raised it up in front of her face. She inspected the glass and the tea inside, making sure it looked OK to drink.

"See, isn't this nice, two friends sitting having tea," Helena smiled.

"We're not friends, I actually hate you," Kim told her.

She took a small sip of tea and immediately spit it back into the glass.

"Ugh…. this is ice cold," she cried.

"Whoops, must be the poison," Helena said.

Kim immediately made eye contact with her.

"It's called a joke Kim, calm down. I'll try to have it warm for you next time."

"There won't be a next time. If I wasn't so tired I'd have already killed you for breaking into my house again."

"Why do you assume I broke in?"

"Because you did?"

Helena sucked her teeth at her answer.

"Anyway, can we talk?" she asked ignoring Kim's claim.

"What is wrong with you?" Kim asked, "Is there seriously something wrong with your head?"

"You wouldn't know it but that's actually incredibly ironic for *you* to be asking *me*," she laughed.

"What?"

"Nothing nothing, so Joey though…"

"Joey? What about him?" Kim asked.

"I don't trust him, the way he left the other day, it was just unsettling don't you think?"

"Who are you to speak about trust and unsettling presence? You literally stalk me."

"Kim I'm not stalking you. Look, focus. He seemed awfully into the pictures of your parents, asked a gang of questions, and then just dipped out, that wasn't odd to you?"

"He lost his parents too, he probably just got emotional for a second. Besides I've known him for years..."

"People change though, right? That's what you told the guy at the mini mart last week," Helena reminded her.

Kim was still uncomfortable with her knowledge of the happening.

"What do you want, what are you trying to say?" she asked.

Helena stood and walked over to Kim's fridge. She pulled the framed photograph of her foster parents down and stared at it.

"I'm just sayin be careful, watch yourself around him," she said.

Kim stood up, snatched the frame from her, and returned it back to its place.

"He's fine," she said, cutting her eyes at her, "I doubt I'll ever even see him again."

Helena shook her head as if disappointed in Kim's lack of concern.

"Just lookin out for you Kim," she said.

"Don't. I got me," she hissed back.

Helena rolled her eyes. Kim grabbed both glasses from the table, poured out the cold tea left in them, and dropped them into the sink.

"Get out. You're giving me a headache and I need to get ready for work."

"Glad to see one less hour of sleep hasn't made you any nastier, certainly hasn't made you any sweeter either, but you know..."

Kim turned and eyed her furiously. Helena threw her hands up surrendering and made her way to the door.

"Love you Kim!" she called halfway outside.

"Shut the door!" Kim commanded her.

~

Kim poked at her salad as she sat at her desk, twirling her fork in the bowl as she stared into space.

"Kim, you OK?" William leaned over.

She was getting tired of being asked that question. While she wouldn't dare let anyone else know it because she knew it would only open up more questions, she wasn't, she was beat. She was constantly tired, constantly thinking about whether she was being followed or watched, and racking her mind daily about decisions she believed she was going to have to make soon.

"Yeah," she sighed.

She dropped her fork into her bowl and buried her face in her hands.

"You don't seem OK..."

"Will, I'm fine. I'm just tired."

"Tired? You had the whole day off yesterday, which by the way covering for you wasn't easy. What happened?" he asked in a hushed tone.

"The morning just started out rough and I knew it was only gonna get worse so I just stayed home."

William stared at her in awe. He couldn't understand how she showed such a lack of concern for even showing up. He couldn't grasp how she didn't fear repercussions.

"Kim you're on thin ice..." he warned her.

"For what?" she said, lifting her head up.

"For never showing up on time, and not showing up at all sometimes." he leaned closer and spoke softer, "The boss has started to notice your absences. There's only so much covering we can do for you."

"You don't have to cover for me," she told him, "I appreciate it but I'll be fine."

"How are you so confident you won't get fired?"

"I'm not. I'm confident that with or without this job I'll be OK."

Max suddenly speed walked up to the two of them. He pulled a chair out from the desk behind them and sat it directly between them.

"The layoff rumors are back on the floor," he said breathing heavily.

Kim rolled her eyes at this and went back to twirling her fork in her salad. William's eyes got huge as he turned and looked at Kim.

"How many? What departments?" he asked.

"No word on that yet," Max heaved.

William let out a sigh of despair.

"You two show up every day on time and work your tails off. I'm sure neither of you have anything to worry about," Kim mumbled.

They both turned and stared at her.

"And what about you?" William asked.

"They'll fire me or I'll continue to be the least productive worker this building has ever seen, that's it," she said, finally sticking a tomato into her mouth.

"But.... you need the job Kim, how are you gonna..."

"I don't," she snapped, "I really don't. All this hellhole does is pile more stress on top of what's already a really stressful life I'm living. Honestly, I'd love if they gave me the boot right now. I've had enough of these fear tactics they're using. Always threatening to let people go so everyone tightens up and over works themselves."

William and Max sat quietly afraid to say anything. They had both known Kim long enough to know once upset or annoyed she was not to be reasoned with, you just shut up and listen.

"I honestly don't know why I'm still here," Kim added.

Her time spent in the building only served to cover where she really made her money. She didn't really need it and at times believed even as a cover up it was useless. She believed so long as she didn't try to dump hundreds of thousands of dollars into a bank account one day, she would ever actually be checked. She came off as too normal. Nothing more or less than anyone else making their money.

However, what truly worried her the most was Cindy. She knew if Cindy began to notice she was staying home every day she would start asking questions. She didn't need that. For this reason, no matter how bad she wanted to quit, no matter how bad she believed she could and still remain safe, she wouldn't.

A look of complete misery rested upon her face as she continued playing with her food, only occasionally taking a bite. Max slowly backed away to his own desk as William retreated to his.

~

"Cin, can you get this in?" Kim shouted as she turned into the living room struggling with her earring again.

Cindy hopped up from the couch shaking her head.

"Wear them more and it won't be so hard," she told her.

Kim bent down to her level and sighed.

"Honestly I don't even know why I'm doing this. I should've never agreed to go."

The doorbell then rang, echoing throughout the house.

"Too late now," Cindy laughed as she dropped back on the couch behind her.

"Have fun," she smiled.

Kim flashed an unamused smirk at her.

"We'll be back in an hour or two."

"Alright, love you."

"Love you too," Kim said, making her way to the door.

She opened it slowly hoping she would see someone else on the other side, but it was exactly who she expected it to be. LuLu stood at the door wearing a white sleeveless strapless blouse and jeans that hugged her curves.

Kim wore a long sleeved jean jacket on top of a white tank top and white jeans.

"You look nice," LuLu smiled.

"I need to change then," Kim said, turning around.

LuLu quickly grabbed her.

"Oh stop, you look fine, don't worry. We're gone sweetie!" LuLu shouted to Cindy.

Kim locked the door behind herself.

"Look I don't really do clubs so…" Kim began.

"It's just a little hangout spot Kim," she told her as they walked to the car.

Kim didn't trust her; LuLu was a very fun loving person and she herself just wasn't. Their ideas of hanging out were very different.

"Two hours at the most," Kim reminded her.

"Oh c'mon, you're gonna love it."

She was pretty sure she wouldn't, and the further they drove she became even more sure she wouldn't. She saw the traffic on the way there and soon became certain LuLu was taking her to a little more than a hangout spot. She began to hear music that was playing so loud it could be heard blocks away. She eventually saw the bright red neon sign on the building of which the music was coming from.

"The Red Devil Night Club," the sign read.

It was then Kim knew she was going to deeply despise the rest of the night.

Kim looked at LuLu without a word. LuLu read her face; she knew she wasn't happy.

"I know it's a club but it's not like a bad one," she cried.

Kim just continued to stare at her blankly. LuLu parked and smiled at Kim, trying to lighten her up.

"We don't have to stay that long. C'mon," she said, getting out of the car.

Kim slowly followed suit. The music instantly grew louder without the shell of the car to mask it. She could only imagine how horrible it must be inside.

LuLu's eyes had lit up, she was already enjoying herself just standing outside. She rushed up to the door as Kim slowly trailed behind her. Their IDs were checked at the door and they were let inside.

"Oh you've got to be kidding me," Kim whispered to herself as she looked around.

The place looked twice as big on the inside as it did on the outside. It was packed full of people all talking, laughing, screaming, and dancing. There were several bars and a huge stage positioned in the middle towards the back. The entire place reeked of sweat, alcohol, and smoke. The air felt polluted as Kim breathed it in and out of her nose.

She couldn't hear herself think. Between the constant chatter, laughter, chanting, and ear blistering music, Kim was sure she would be deaf by the end of the night as a massive migraine had already started attacking her.

It was unbelievably crowded. They had surely passed the building's maximum occupancy. She hated crowds but this was more than a crowd, it was a mob, an army, a storm of everything she despised. She turned and looked at LuLu in disgust. She knew what she had done but simply shrugged in Kim's direction.

A huddle of five girls suddenly rushed the two of them and crowded around LuLu greeting her with several high pitched squeals. LuLu returned this gesture as Kim stood looking at them all in amazement. She figured they were LuLu's friends from school. She couldn't understand how they had so much energy to expend on just a greeting.

They talked amongst themselves for a few seconds smiling and laughing about things Kim couldn't make out over the noise surrounding them. LuLu quickly turned around suddenly remembering Kim was even there. She introduced her.

Kim extended her hand out but the girls, all of whom held drinks in their hands, only smiled and greeted her in unison with, "Nice to meet you."

One of the girls, the shortest of the bunch pointed in the direction of where they had came and whispered something to LuLu. She nodded and began following her and the girls after gesturing Kim to do the same.

The five of them, plus LuLu began swiftly cutting through the crowds of people as Kim struggled to keep up with them. She bumped into people, spilled drinks, interrupted conversations, and split dancing couples. She pushed and pulled bodies out of her path and ducked under several arms before realizing she had lost LuLu and her friends. She couldn't even tell which direction she had come from as everything around her looked the same. She stood standing still like a lost child in a sea of strangers.

She stood on her toes hoping to spot LuLu, but to no avail. What she did see was a bar close to her with an abundance of open seats. She squeezed her way through apologizing for grabbing and moving people out of her way as she moved to the bar. Once she had made it through she sat on one of the stools, spun around, and scanned again for LuLu who was still nowhere to be found.

While she couldn't believe it, she had also expected the night to go as such. She wasn't entirely sure why LuLu had even invited her. She knew if LuLu truly wanted to enjoy herself, she would have to do it with someone besides her, like the girls she had just disappeared with. Kim simply wasn't one to enjoy a night out at a club with.

She pressed on her forehead which had been throbbing since they entered the building. The sound assaulting her ears from every direction was killing her.

"What can I get you ma'am?" a voice from behind her shouted.

Kim turned around and met eyes with Helena standing behind the bar with her patented smile.

Kim's face scrunched up seeing this.

"There's no way you're old enough to be in here," Kim said cutting her eyes at her.

Helena shrugged with a grin.

"Didn't know you were the clubbing type K," she said.

"My friend dragged me out here and then went off somewhere with a group of her own friends. I'mma kill her when I find her," Kim grumbled.

"Knowing how capable you are of that, I feel like someone should warn her," Helena laughed.

Kim didn't find her constant poking at her secret funny. However, she was afraid to say anything out of fear of dwelling on the subject too long. She wanted her to forget it.

She looked over the bar at her and again saw she still hadn't changed her clothes. She was still in the same oversized muscle shirt, shorts, and hat as she had been in every other time Kim had seen her. It was odd, but what truly puzzled her though was that as many times as she had seen her in the clothes, they never appeared dirty or worn.

"Hey, are you homeless?" Kim asked her.

"What do you mean?"

"You've been wearing those same clothes for days."

She smiled big bracing herself against the bar.

"Let's just say it's all you gave me to work with."

She held a pompous expression as the words passed over her lips.

"What?" Kim questioned.

"Nothing nothing," she shouted quickly changing the subject, "c'mon K, go mingle, meet you a guy or two. You look great, I saw a few of them checking you out."

"I don't mingle, I don't know anyone in this place and I don't want to."

"Well, don't look now but here comes two people you know *very* well," she said, eyeing to Kim's right.

She turned and saw Aaliyah and another light brown skinned Hispanic woman she recognized walking towards her. They were both dressed in all black. Helena made her way down to the other end of the bar out of Kim's sight.

Aaliyah and the woman each sat down at Kim's sides. They made no eye contact nor did either even turn to acknowledge her. All three pulled out their cell phones and pretended to text as they spoke.

"What are y'all doing here?" Kim asked them.

"What are you doing here, you don't club," the Hispanic woman responded.

Charlotte, the fourth assassin of The Pool, a quick witted, no nonsense type who also served as The Pool's medic whenever need be. She had a light brown skin tone with dark brown hair which she usually had pulled into a ponytail. She was around the same height and weight as both Kim and Aaliyah. She spoke with a slight accent, occasionally mixing English and Spanish when she spoke. Her fiery personality made her hard to reason with as she wasn't one to compromise. Aaliyah and she were partners, although they often butted heads as her hard personality didn't always mesh well with Aaliyah's easy going one.

"Friend dragged me out," Kim responded.

"You have a friend?" Aaliyah snickered.

"Funny." Kim smirked, "What are y'all doing here?"

"Contract," Charlotte said, "we saw you and thought Terrance sent you as backup."

"Do you *need* backup?" Kim asked.

"Of course not," Charlotte assured her.

"But it couldn't hurt to have a lookout," Aaliyah added.

As much as Kim didn't want any part of The Pool, at the moment she was still a part of it. She would be wrong to deny them help if they were asking for it.

"Terrance would flip if he knew I got involved with a contract my name wasn't on," Kim said.

"So we're not gonna tell him," Aaliyah said.

"Did you find your target?" Kim asked.

"The DJ on stage right now," Aaliyah said.

Kim glanced over and saw the man on stage. He was a black, clean cut man, with a small frame. He was wearing a bright neon yellow jacket that could be seen from a mile away. She would normally consider him an easy kill to confirm but the setting made things a bit more difficult.

"Why here?" Kim asked, "Can it wait until he leaves, there's a lot of eyes in here."

"He's only in Joy City tonight, we only have this location. We could tail him from here but he'll for sure be protected. Getting him in here on that stage is our best bet," Charlotte explained.

"Plan?" Kim asked.

"I've got the building layout. I'm gonna get to the power, shut it off and by the time they get the lights back on he'll be dead," Aaliyah explained.

"Let's move before he does," Charlotte said.

Aaliyah grabbed Kim's hand under the cover of the bar and opened it. She handed Kim an earpiece.

"Give us five minutes to get into place, let us know of anything you see."

Aaliyah and Charlotte disappeared into the crowd. Kim dropped her head and looked at the earpiece in her hand.

"Help them out K, they might need you," Helena smiled now back in front of her.

She didn't want to be involved, she wanted out, but the earpiece was already in her hand. She put it in, tucked her chain into her shirt, and got up from the bar to move closer to the stage.

"Good luck, don't kill him too hard!" Helena called out to her.

Kim pushed her way through the crowd again this time omitting the apologies she was handing out earlier. It seemed the gaps in between the people were getting tighter. The music was also growing unbearably loud as she inched closer towards the giant speakers that lined the bottom of the stage. It all only made her more sour towards LuLu for dragging her out.

Suddenly the music's volume dipped as the DJ came over the loudspeaker. All eyes in the club focused on him.

"It's gettin late, we bout to set the mood! Fellas grab you a lady, and ladies grab on to that fool's wallet!" he shouted.

The music immediately pumped back up even louder than it had before as the lights turned off. A few massive spotlights hanging high above panned wildly back and forth illuminating the club's floors.

Kim grabbed her head and gritted her teeth in pain as the music pounded against her head.

"Kim, you alright?" she heard Charlotte ask through her earpiece.

"I-I'm fine. Aaliyah the lights, was that you?" she spit out through several grunts.

"The lights?" Aaliyah asked, "What? I just got to the power switch I haven't touched anything."

"Ay dios mio Kim, it's a club, they just cut the lights, calm down." Charlotte told her, "Aaliyah, the lights are off except for the spotlight and strobes hanging in the rafters."

"Alright, I can cut everything whenever you're ready?"

"Kim, are we clear?" Charlotte asked.

She was struggling to hear them. She pressed the earpiece deeper into her ear.

"Wait, what's even the plan?" Kim asked.

"Ugh…." Charlotte sighed annoyed, "Look up chica, on your left behind the second light."

Kim looked up and saw her on the upper level where the light fixtures hung.

"When she cuts the lights, be careful down there, they're gonna scramble," she told Kim.

The noise was beating her down, she could barely comprehend what she was hearing or seeing. Normally she would be the one issuing the orders to them but the headache she was battling barely

112

allowed her to think at the moment.

"Kim?!" Charlotte cried through the earpiece.

"I got it!" she yelled back, "Go ahead!"

She looked at Charlotte who had pulled a scarf up over her mouth. They made eye contact and nodded to each other. She pulled a small handgun from a small pouch at her side and focused on the DJ on stage.

"Aaliyah, get ready," Charlotte whispered.

Kim watched as Charlotte pulled the gun up to aim just as her eyes caught something moving on the same platform behind her. It was a figure of a man.

"Whoa whoa whoa, Charlotte stop!" Kim yelled.

"What?!" she froze and pulled the gun back to her chest.

The figure spun the spotlight around into Charlotte's face. She stumbled backwards as the bright light blinded her. The sudden shift of the spotlight got the attention of most of the crowd on the floor. They all glanced up at Charlotte shielding her eyes with one hand, and a gun clearly visible in the other.

Kim heard a few gasps and screams from around her as more and more eyes shifted upwards.

"Oh my god! she's got a gun!" a voice cried out.

Several more alarmed clubbers cried out as well, stirring the panic.

"Aaliyah, cut everything now!" Kim commanded.

In an instant it was pitch black in the building,

only the light of cell phone screens, the glow of lighters, and a small luminescence of the door leading outside provided light to see. The screams of panic grew even louder.

"Charlotte, get down now, there's someone up there!" Kim yelled.

She was suddenly knocked to the ground by a mass of fleeing bodies. Most were heading towards the exit in the opposite direction of the stage. She pushed herself back up to her feet again as the panic continued inside the club.

"Yo, what's happening out there?!" Aaliyah asked.

"Charlotte?! Charlotte?!" Kim called.

It was too dark to see anything from where she was. She looked up to the lights where she had been standing hoping to see something. She was then pushed by another fleeing person, this time knocking her earpiece out of her ear. She cursed under her breath knowing she had no chance of finding it in the dark as hundreds of people circled around her in fear.

She grabbed the shoulder of a random person passing by and held on to them as they made for the door. There were people running every which way, people on the ground, people standing on top of the bar, it was complete hysteria. She was determined to get out but then remembered she hadn't come alone. She had to find LuLu, but in the dark couldn't imagine how it would be possible. She let go of the person she was holding onto and stopped in her tracks. She squinted as if it would help her see anything at all, but she couldn't see her own hand in front of her face.

At that moment someone ran over her. Instinctively, she grabbed onto the person and pulled them down with her. She fell on her back and felt the weight of a body land on top of her. She could hear feet continuing to shuffle by her as she laid on the ground. She covered her head hoping no one would step or trip over her. Suddenly the spotlights flickered back on and a voice came over the loud speaker urging the crowd to calm down. The lights, while only flashing for a second, provided enough light for Kim to see who she was lying under.

She couldn't see a face but recognized the bright yellow jacket the DJ had been wearing. He had reacted to the frenzy and in a panic ran right into Kim, knocking her over and landing on top of her.

Without a second thought she pulled her hair pick from her waist, gripped it in her fist and stuck the bladed end of it in the man's throat. He grabbed her hand as she pulled it from right to the left until he ceased struggling and fell completely onto her.

She rolled his body off of hers, got up and looked back up at where Charlotte had been standing. She could now slightly see from the flickering of the spotlights. She didn't see Charlotte but did see a figure standing above, watching as hundreds of people continued to scatter around the club floor. It was the same figure she had seen point the light at Charlotte.

She squinted looking at the figure trying to get a glimpse of a face but could only see half of one. It was familiar, the jaw structure, the slim build, the messy unkempt hair. A knot formed in her stomach as she was able to put a name to the profile. It was Joey.

Joey? she asked herself.

Another bump from someone pushed her in the direction of the door. She stumbled to keep herself on her feet. She stood upright and made a dash for the exit. She bulldogged through a crowd of several people still in a panic before making it outside into the parking lot. As she took a moment to catch her breath she looked down and noticed her white shirt had been stained with blood. She quickly buttoned up her jacket and looked around for LuLu.

She moved back slightly towards the door attempting to peek inside as countless bodies spilled out into the parking lot. She eventually saw LuLu squeezing her way through the door with a look of terror on her face. As soon as she was outside she panned left and right. Kim quickly ran up to her, grabbed her by her arm, and pulled her away from the club's door. They ran back to the car and got inside. They were both out of breath as they looked at each other in shock.

"Where'd you go?" LuLu asked.

"Where'd *I* go? Where were *you*? As soon as your friends showed up you disappeared."

"We were barely ten feet from the door," she breathed.

"Whatever, c'mon, let's go before we get stuck in here," Kim said, scanning the lot.

"Did you see what happened up there?" LuLu asked as she turned on the engine.

"No, I was sitting at the bar. Next thing I knew people started screaming and the lights went off so I just ran for the exit."

The parking lot was full of people. Several had already gotten in their cars and were attempting to leave as well. The overall panic was still present outside but much calmer than it had been inside.

As LuLu swerved through the parking lot Kim watched as people continued to push and shove their way out of the club's entrance.

"Sorry Kim, I know you didn't really wanna come and it kinda turned into..."

"Don't worry about it," Kim said, cutting her apology short, "just glad we got outta there."

Their ride home was mostly silent aside from LuLu apologizing a few more times. Kim continuously assured her it was OK and that she wasn't blaming her. Kim's mind was somewhere else though. She was at a loss. Was Charlotte OK, why would Joey have even been up there, why would he interfere? Her mind was racing.

~

They made it home and Kim told LuLu she was going to go straight to sleep. She instead left and immediately headed to the pool hall.

She arrived, pulled the door open, and slid inside. Charlotte was sitting on the edge of one of the pool tables. She appeared to be fine. Kim let out a sigh of relief seeing that she wasn't hurt.

"You OK?" Kim asked.

"Yeah I'm good, are you..."

"Kim!" Terrance stuck his head out the back room and glared at her, "what happened?!"

Both Kim and Charlotte jumped at his entrance. He sounded like a father about to scold his child.

"I don't know," she responded with an attitude.

He stomped over to her.

"You don't know? Nah you know something. Aaliyah said she asked you about the contract yesterday, and you said no, so why were you there?"

Aaliyah poked her head out from the back room Terrance had exited from.

"I was out with a friend if it's any of your business," Kim replied, shooting him a glare back.

"Coincidently, at the same place and time they had a contract that night, really, you want me to believe that?"

"I don't care if you believe it, it's the truth," she fired back.

"Hey hey, relax OK," Charlotte said stepping in between them.

Kim pushed her aside.

"You think I went there to tag in on the contract? I've been beggin you to keep me off of them for weeks now, why would I suddenly want in on one now?"

"If you didn't wanna get involved why did you? If you didn't wanna be a part of it you should've stayed out of it!"

"We asked her to," Aaliyah stepped out of the room, "she was there and we thought it couldn't hurt to have backup."

Terrance looked at her and then at Charlotte for conformation. She nodded in agreeance.

"Doesn't excuse it, you should've known better, you been doin this for too long, you know better," he growled, turning his attention back to Kim.

"You can't be serious..." she mumbled under her breath.

"You jeopardized the whole contract, let money walk right out the door."

"Hey, she was helping, he got away but we can track him down again if..." Charlotte began.

"He didn't get away," Kim interrupted her.

All three of them turned to her.

"When the lights went out he ran straight into me. I killed him right there."

"In a club full of people?!" Terrance exclaimed.

"Who were running in panic, in a dark room, no one saw anything!"

"Kim, that's careless and you know it!" he barked at her.

"More careless than letting him go?! He saw Charlotte pointing a gun at him, so did half the club!" Kim fired back.

The two were heating up. The tension in the pool hall was high. Both Aaliyah and Charlotte had moved close to them wondering when the right time to pull them apart would be.

"He saw you?" Terrance asked looking to Charlotte.

"Oh you didn't tell him the best part?" Kim

asked her, "A civilian nearly blinded her and who knows what he was gonna do to her after that. So I told Aaliyah to kill the lights."

"So you're giving orders on a contract your name's not even on?!"

Kim squeezed her forehead between her thumb and fingers.

"Oh my god, you're not even listening!"

She took her voice up several tones until she was practically shaking as she spoke.

"Had I not interfered she would probably have gotten caught and detained or worse on top of the target getting away! How are you flipping this on me?!"

"Because you weren't supposed to be involved, you know how dangerous that is. They'd already planned a way to confirm the kill and adding you last minute threw everything off!"

"What?! Are you insane?!" she cried, "I don't even wanna do this anymore! You've been begging me to stay and now when I actually do something to help you freak out on me?!"

"Are you insane?! You killed a man on an open club floor, and then just left, didn't even double back to check on your partners! You're careless, just like your father was!"

Kim's face full of anger quickly turned to one full of hurt.

"He always thought he was smarter than he was, thought he didn't have to step the same way as everyone else and that's why he's dead now! You're just like him, hardheaded and impulsive, if you don't wanna do this anymore then don't! Leave! But don't go putting the rest of us at risk! We all work too hard trying to keep this thing going in his and your mother's names but if you don't care enough about it anymore then just go and don't come back, I'm not gonna let you or anything else be the downfall of what we built in here!"

Kim had shrunk. She couldn't believe him. What he had let come out of his mouth about her father, his best friend, his partner.

She looked at him horrified, like he was a stranger. He glared back at her slowly catching his breath as Aaliyah and Charlotte shared horrified gazes.

Kim slowly backed away, never taking her eyes off Terrance until she was able to slide out the door. She closed it softly and began a slow walk down the path that led out to the dead end road. She walked with her head down, pouting as she fought back tears. Terrance's words had cut her deep.

"Well, he took that well," Helena said sarcastically as she came from behind Kim.

Kim ignored her.

"You'd think he'd be a bit more grateful. He could've lost Charlotte and The Pool entirely tonight had it not been for you."

Kim again ignored her. Helena noticed the sad look on her face and matched it for a second.

"Hey cheer up, this is what you wanted right? You're finally free, you can do whatever you want now," she smiled.

Kim refused to pick her head up from the

121

ground. She just continued to walk in silence. Helena's smile faded.

"You know, I love you Kim, I really do, but I gotta tell you, sometimes you're depressing as..."

"Shut up!" Kim exploded at her.

She had turned around completely and gotten into her face.

"Whoa Kim..."

"No! I'm sick of you! I'm sick of you stalking me, sick of you commenting on every little thing that's none of your business, sick of you breaking into my house, sick of hearing your voice! I don't know who you are or how you know me, and I really don't care anymore, but I'm sick of seeing you everywhere!"

Kim grabbed her arm and yanked her close to her. She pulled her hair pick from her waist and pointed the blade directly between Helena's eyes less than an inch from her face.

"Stay away from me. If I see you again, I'm going to kill you, that's a threat."

She retracted the blade, tucked the pick back at her side, and pushed her away. She looked at Helena who for the first time since she had met her showed an emotion other than happiness or excitement. There was genuine fear and sadness in her eyes. No smile, no laugh, no bright eyed glare as she stood looking back at her; she just looked hurt. Kim turned away from her and continued her walk in silence.

Chapter 6

Kim II

Kim rolled out of bed and stumbled into her bathroom. She was beat. Another sleepless night she had spent thinking for way too long about way too much. The weekend had come and gone, and both nights were restless for her.

She flicked the lights on and caught a glimpse of herself in the mirror. She looked awful. She stood staring at her reflection contemplating if going to work was even worth it. She was pretty sure she was out of The Pool so maintaining a cover up job was no longer a priority. It was practically pointless but she knew she still wasn't yet prepared for Cindy's questions. So, she began her morning routine as normal and headed downstairs.

As she made it to the bottom of the staircase, she saw a glass of tea resting on the table and heard the light hum of the TV in the next room.

Kim ground her teeth together and frowned. She pulled her pick from her side and clinched it in a fist with the blade sticking out from in between her middle and ring finger. She stomped around the corner but found Cindy sitting on the couch with one eyebrow raised at her aggressive entrance. Kim quickly retracted the blade back and hid the pick behind her back.

"Oh hey, didn't think you'd be up this early?"

"Couldn't sleep," she said.

"Oh OK, well, I'm about to leave for work, keep the doors locked OK, and don't answer it for anyone?"

Cindy looked at her puzzled. She leaned forward from the couch and cut her eyes at Kim.

"Why have you been so worried about that lately?" she asked.

"Locking up?"

"Not just that, you've just been acting really paranoid lately."

Kim was normally quick on her feet and could create believable lies at the drop of a hat. The exception was when it came to Cindy. This was partly because of how much she hated lying to her in the first place, but also the fact that Cindy was not easily lied to; she was too smart.

"Just.... please, I just wanna make sure you're safe," Kim whispered.

Her voice was so weak, so pathetic. It was practically begging Cindy not to ask anything else but just go with it. Cindy picked up on the tone in her voice and submitted. She fell back into the couch.

"Alright," she said.

Kim disappeared around the corner and out the door.

~

"Need help with something?" Max asked.

His voice was timid, he was afraid.

Kim sat at her desk with her elbows up and her face buried in her hands. She slowly picked her head up and glared at him.

"No Max," she groaned, dropping her head back down.

"Well.... you have any plans for lunch? Me and Will were gonna..."

"No thanks.... I'm fine," she said.

"You sure?"

"Max please.... I just need to be alone right now," she pleaded.

He quietly backed away.

She felt like she was cracking. Stress was consuming her. While she technically had gotten what she wanted, an exit from The Pool, she struggled to find herself happy. She believed it was the way she exited, practically kicked out. It wasn't that she expected or even would've liked for them to have thrown her some sort of going away party, but to be told to just leave didn't sit well with her. On top of that she still didn't believe she had done anything wrong; she was of the mindset she had made the smartest decision amongst the fray. Six long years she gave to The Pool, seeing things some would consider to be the fuel of nightmares, all to be just told to leave.

There was also Helena, whose presence still

made her uncomfortable. She hadn't seen her the entire weekend after snapping on her outside the pool hall. *Maybe she finally got the message* she thought. Regardless of whether she would ever show up again or not, Kim still couldn't help but wonder about the girl, who she was, how she knew her, how she always ended up wherever Kim was, how she knew everything she knew. The girl was just a complete mystery. Her presence felt so innocent but what she knew, how she carried herself, her mannerisms, they were so defined, so real.

"Our supervisor is coming on the floor to take a head count, make sure you look busy when he comes by," William whispered leaning into Kim's ear.

"A headcount?!" Kim cried.

Her voice was much louder than his, she practically shouted her response. This took William by surprise, his eyes widened and his mouth fell open.

"Are we slaves?!" she asked aloud.

"Kim.... shhh," he urged her.

"No, do you hear yourself? It shouldn't be like this, we shouldn't be slaving for people while they sit back making dollars to our pennies. And now they're gonna come in here to write someone up for going to get a cup of coffee outside their break time? This place is hell!"

Most of the floor was staring at her in shock. Her outburst only got louder as she continued to speak.

"Kim?! Calm down," he spoke through his

teeth.

She looked at him in amazement.

"How? How are you OK with this? Being here every day and working so much harder than those above you while they reap the benefits. How?"

He had no answer. Kim shook her head at his inability to respond. She looked over and made eye contact with a few onlookers who all immediately dropped their heads back down to their work.

"I can't be in this building right now," Kim said, her tone settling, "I'm taking an early lunch. If they fire me, call me so I know not to waste my time coming back."

She stood and walked off with nearly all eyes on the floor on her. As she made her way towards the building's main exit, she caught stares from passing co-workers. In return as she passed by, she mean mugged them all back.

She got to the main desk that stood just beyond the main exit. There was no one at the desk to sign her out so she just walked straight outside. The cool air was refreshing as it brushed against her face. It was nothing like the overly chilling air that beat down on her from the vents inside the building, just cool crisp fresh air. She basked in it for a minute breathing in deeply through her nose and releasing out her mouth. She felt she was about at her end with her day job. Much like The Pool, it served no purpose anymore.

Two honks of a car horn suddenly grabbed her attention. She scanned the parking lot and her eyes immediately locked on Pedro's purple eyesore of a vehicle. She sighed deeply, annoyed, knowing what was coming. She wished she could've pretended not to see him but it was too late.

He rolled his window down, leaned out the car, and waved her down. She started a slow shameful walk towards the car. She didn't want to talk about what had happened Saturday but she knew they would. He would pry like always until she opened up about it.

She walked around to the passenger side, opened the door, and slid inside.

"This car gets uglier the closer you get to it," she said, avoiding eye contact.

He laughed at her remark.

"What's up?" he asked.

"Nothin. How bout you?"

"I was just out here and thought I'd stop by and..." he paused as Kim began eyeing him.

Pedro never just stopped by to see Kim. In fact, Terrance disapproved of The Pool members having contact with each other outside of the pool hall or when they were on contract together, he thought it too risky. Pedro would only stop by to see Kim when he needed something from her. He knew she knew this.

"OK OK, you know why I'm here."

He reached into the center console and pulled out a folder full of papers.

"The targets gotta be confirmed dead by the end of next week or we'll lose him completely. We're trying to get information so we can try to confirm the kill as soon as possible. Look, I'm trying to pull

Aaliyah but she's already up to her neck in contracts. Charlotte too. I know you said you don't wanna..."

"I'm not in The Pool anymore," she interrupted.

His jaw dropped.

"W-what?"

"At least I don't think I am. Figured they would've told you."

"Told me what?"

"Saturday, I messed up…. I guess. I killed a running target, after someone interfered and things just went bad."

"What? Who interfered? Where was this?"

"I-I don't know. It's not important, just know that I'm out," she shrugged.

He put his hand over his chin and fell deep into his thoughts for a few seconds. Kim wanted to just get out but knew more questions were coming. He wouldn't let her off that easily.

"You really quit huh?" he said placing the papers in the side of the door.

"No actually, Terrance kinda kicked me out."

"He kicked you out?"

"It's a long stupid story OK. Ask Aaliyah or Charlotte, they were there. I'm sick of talking about it really, sick of thinking about it, and I'm just glad it's behind me now."

Pedro looked hurt, betrayed. Kim was his partner and while he knew why she believed she had to leave and respected her decision, it still hurt to see her walk away. She had trained him, taught him just about everything he knew.

"I'm sorry..." Kim told him.

"It's cool, we'll be good…. do what you gotta do."

"Thanks," she said.

They sat in silence for a moment, making sure to either look straight or away from the other. Eye contact felt like a trap to them both at the moment.

Kim felt slightly guilty; she knew Pedro was a victim in the situation. He was losing his partner because she couldn't handle it anymore. She appreciated him so much for his understanding and support of her decision, but she knew deep down he was hurt by it.

"Well, I only got forty-five minutes for lunch so…"

"Yeah, I'll…. see you around," he said.

She opened the door and stepped out with a huff of air. As she started to walk away she caught the window rolling down out the corner of her eye. She took a step back and bent down to make eye contact with him.

"Love you Kim," he grinned.

She flashed a small smile back at him.

"Love you too Pedro. Be safe."

"Always," he said, as he rolled the window up and drove off.

~

"Cin, I'm home!" Kim shouted, closing the door behind her.

"We're up here Kim!" LuLu called.

130

"Lu?!"

"Yep!"

Cindy rounded the corner and came down the stairs

"You called her over?" Kim asked.

"No. She showed up, saw my room, and started making a big deal over it not being spotless so she said she'd help me clean it up."

"Help? So why are you coming down?"

"I didn't say I'd help her," she shrugged.

"Brat," Kim laughed.

"I'm gonna heat up some tea," Cindy said heading over to the pantry.

LuLu came from around the corner and started down the stairs herself.

"Hey Kim, I'm sorry, that girl's room was a disaster. I had to do something."

"Well she definitely wasn't gonna do it herself so I appreciate it."

"No problem, what's up, how was work?" she said, stopping at the bottom of the stairs.

Kim turned and looked at Cindy still digging in the pantry.

"Ummm…. actually I wanna talk to you about that," she whispered.

"Everything OK?" she asked.

Kim shushed her, gently pushing her back upstairs.

"Cin make enough for us too, we'll be back down in a minute."

"Alright," she hollered back.

"Kim, I hate that stuff."

"Shhh," Kim hushed her again.

Kim pushed and shoved her all the way upstairs until they were in her room. She closed the door leaving it slightly cracked.

"What's going on?" LuLu asked worried.

"Work," Kim whispered.

LuLu raised an eyebrow.

"I'm thinkin about quitting," Kim said, squinting her eyes.

"Why?"

"I'm just really stressed out and that jobs only making things worse and.... I just don't know. I'm really unhappy just being there every day."

"Kim how are you gonna pay your bills?" she asked.

"I have a plan, don't worry about that, the issue is her." Kim said, pointing downstairs, "If she starts noticing me not going to work and starts asking questions..."

"Well wait, what's the plan?" LuLu asked.

Kim scrunched her face up realizing she hadn't come up with a lie to cover herself.

"It's kinda personal," Kim told her.

LuLu gasped.

"Are you.... escorting?" she asked horrified.

"What?! No?!" she cried pushing LuLu's arm.

She reacted as if offended by LuLu's guess. As if the way she actually acquired her money was any cleaner of an act.

"I just can't talk about it right now to anyone, especially not her," Kim explained.

"OK, well, whatever this plan is, are you

positive it's gonna bring in enough money to support you both?"

Kim knew she could only say so much while still keeping the secret. It was hopeless. She dropped her head as a small frown came over her face.

"Never mind," she said softly.

The disappointment in her voice was evident.

"Kim, do whatever you have to do to be happy but just remember, you got two mouths to feed at the end of the day."

"Yeah..." Kim whispered looking back at the door.

LuLu grabbed her by the hand.

"I know you'll do what's right for her and yourself. Don't sweat it."

Kim flashed a cheap smile.

"And whenever you're ready, whatever this plan is, if it works let me know about it, so I can start working on all this debt," LuLu said exiting the room.

Kim rolled her eyes at her request. She was certain if she knew the plan she was speaking of she would want no part of even hearing about it.

~

"Cin grab a jacket before you leave it's gonna be pretty chilly today!" Kim shouted, heading down the stairs.

She was running late for work again. Having no real reason to maintain her job anymore left her with less motivation than she required to care about being on time. The only reason she was still getting up at all was because she still hadn't quite figured out how she would dodge Cindy's questions.

"I don't know where it is!" she shouted from her bed.

"Ugh…. isn't it in the closet down here?!"

"I don't know!"

"Ugh…" Kim groaned under her breath.

Kim swung open the door to the coat closet and three large duffle bags dropped onto the ground spilling stacks of money onto the floor.

Kim cursed under her breath and quickly beamed her focus to the top of the stairs making sure Cindy hadn't crept out of her room. She had no answer for having bags filled with several thousands of dollars stored in the coat closet. She quickly stuffed the money back in the bags, zipped them up securely and crammed them back into their places. She pulled Cindy's coat out from behind them and rested it over the railing of the stairs.

"It's on the stairs, don't forget it!" she shouted.

She turned around and looked towards the closet deciding if she needed to move the bags. She eventually decided no, she knew Cindy would come home and simply toss her coat on the floor somewhere. This was the reason she had become so comfortable stashing the money there in the first place; she knew she was the only one who ever opened it. Still, it was an unsettling thought. She promised herself she would do something about them soon. She closed the closet door and headed off to work.

~

Kim sat at her desk side eyeing William sitting on her left.

"Uhhh.... you OK?" he asked.

Kim's stared at him sideways.

"How do you come here every day so happy? Like every time I think about this place I just wanna jump off a bridge and land on a flagpole."

"Kim, you're overreacting. It's not that bad here. You make it a lot worse for yourself always being late or just not showing up," he laughed.

"Yeah there's a reason I don't show up to this hellhole every day," she remarked, standing up, "I'm goin on lunch."

"Where you headed, I'll roll with you."

"Uhhh…. no, I don't think you wanna do that cause I just might not come back honestly."

William laughed until he caught a glimpse of her face and realized she was serious.

"Kim, we can't keep covering for you..."

"Then don't, don't put yourselves at risk for me. I'll be fine," she said, as she turned away and made her way out the building.

She wasn't particularly hungry, she just needed to get outside. She got in her car and began cruising around the city. It was truly a sight to see in all the worst ways. Some had described it as a place where you could just feel the bad energy in the air. While it was her city, where she was born and raised, she wasn't fond of it and hoped one day she would find a way out, for both herself and Cindy.

She had about forty-five minutes to decide if she was going back for the day. She already knew what she wanted to do but decided to let the time play out and make her final decision then. She eventually found herself parked across the street from a local diner. She figured a glass of tea was all she really needed at the moment.

As she stepped out of her car a high pitch voice called from behind her, "Ball! Ma'am?! Ball?!"

She turned around and saw a group of kids looking in her direction as a basketball bounced towards her. It had bounced just outside the opening of the fenced in courts. She grabbed the ball and flicked it back in the direction of the kids who thanked her and continued their game.

Kim walked up to the fence and ran her fingers across a navy blue plaque tied to it that read,"FoxHound Courts."

Two fenced in full length side by side basketball courts. Kim knew them well. The baby blue perimeter, the orange painted key, and the white lines that cut the entirety of the courts up.

When she was younger she would walk to the courts after school and play on teams of three to five with her foster siblings from The Home. She hadn't really stopped to look at the courts in years but they were just as she remembered them. Cracks and chips in the painted cement, chain linked nets that made the most satisfying sound when a ball passed through them, and a crowd of onlookers lining the sides of the cage. So many memories quickly rushed back through her mind. Heated debates of whether the ball was out of bounds or not, who touched it last, arguments over who would take the last shot, and of course, the time one of her foster brothers rolled his ankle and had to be carried back home by the others. It was familiar. It was comforting to see after all these years the place was still the same.

"Kim?! Hey?!" she heard a voice shout from inside the fence.

Her focus immediately went to the tallest person inside with his hand up as he walked towards her. It was Blake, one of her foster brothers she lived with at The Home. An extremely tall, lanky even, red haired, freckle faced grin, slowly walked towards her.

She cussed under her breath at the sight of him. It wasn't that she didn't want to see him, she just knew she didn't have the time. Blake could be long winded when he got going.

"What are you doing here?" he asked clinging to the fence.

"What are *you* doing here?" she asked back, "You're way too old and too tall to be playin with these kids."

"They're from The Home, they wanted to come play ball so I said I'd take them."

Unlike Kim, Blake embraced growing up in a foster home. He loved the fact he got to meet so many people around his age, grow up with them, and call them his brothers and sisters. Even now as an adult he often went back to meet newer kids and served as a big brother and mentor to them, something he always urged Kim to do as well.

"You still go back there every week huh?"

"Yeah, why don't you?" he asked.

She didn't have an answer truthfully. The last time she could remember having spent any significant time there was when she adopted Cindy about five years ago.

"They miss you Kim. They'd love to have you come back and talk to some of the new kids."

She shook her head no, "I-I don't have much to tell them."

He looked disappointed in her answer. He stepped to the side and opened the gate for her to come in.

"I can't, I only got like thirty minutes for lunch..."

"As if you were actually going back anyway?"

Blake knew Kim hated her job because she told him nearly every time they spoke. What he didn't know was she wasn't always talking about her office job.

Kim shrugged and stepped inside.

"How's the job goin anyway?"

"I think I'm about to quit," she told him.

"And continue to pay bills how?"

"I'll figure it out."

The pair walked down to the opposite side of the court the kids were playing on. Blake picked up a basketball and stood behind the three-point line.

"As in get another job?"

"As in I'll figure it out," she repeated.

Blake shook his head as he took a shot that rimmed in. Kim grabbed the ball and passed it back to him.

"But what's that mean? How are you gonna take care of yourself and Cindy?"

"It's fine. I got it," she assured him.

He shrugged.

"How is Cindy anyway?" he asked as he took another shot that banged off the front of the rim and dropped in.

"She's fine. Broke a kid's nose about a week ago," she said as she pushed the ball back to him.

He caught the ball and froze.

"What? Is she OK?" he asked with widened eyes.

"She's fine. She was doing the right thing believe it or not. She got suspended but she went back today."

"OK..." he said, slightly rattled by her lack of urgency about the matter.

"She's fine really, go on shoot," she told him.

He took a shot that bounced off the side of the rim and into Kim's arms.

"Brick!" she grinned, "Iced you, same old broken shot you had back when we were kids."

"Whatever," he said, rolling his eyes.

They switched places. Kim tucked her chain in and positioned herself behind the line.

"You seen anyone else from The Home recently?" he asked her.

She immediately thought about Joey, homeless, possibly living on the streets somewhere, and then of course, his presence at the nightclub Friday.

"No, no one but LuLu," she said, taking a shot that swished on the chain net.

"Talked to her Saturday or Sunday I think, she said y'all went out and things got kinda ugly." he said, passing the ball back to her.

"Uhhh.... yeah.... I uhhh.... don't actually know what happened. One moment everything was cool, next moment the lights are off and people are runnin out the doors screaming."

"They said the DJ was killed in the whole mess," he added.

"Really, that's crazy," she said as she drained another shot.

He bounced the ball back to her, "Yeah, be careful out there."

"I'm always careful. Besides I don't go out like that as it is. Lu dragged me out that night," she told him.

She sunk a third shot.

"Why not?" he asked.

"Too busy, work," she shrugged.

"The way you talk that's ending soon though."

Kim caught another pass from him.

"It might already be done." she remarked, putting up another perfect shot.

This time Blake held the ball when he retrieved it.

"Already done?" he asked.

"I mean look where I am right now, they'll probably fire me pretty soon for all the times I've been late or no showed. It's just a matter of time."

"And you'll be OK? Like you have a plan if

that happens?" he asked.

Kim glared at him annoyed.

"Yes, I told you, I'm fine. I got it. Ball."

He twisted his lips unsure of her answer but knew how stubborn she was, so he just went with it.

"Step back," he told her.

Kim took a step back and he passed the ball back to her. Still, she easily made the shot and smiled arrogantly at him.

"Only thing missing is you on the ground cryin that you tripped on your shoelace," she teased.

"Whatever," he moaned.

"Yeah yeah," she mocked him, "little sis had you on skates back in the day, it's OK."

He passed the ball back to her with a little more force. She again swished it.

"That's such a nice sound, not that you'd recognize it," she laughed.

He grabbed the ball and squeezed it in between his hands.

"C'mon, ball up," she said, putting her hands out to catch a pass.

He remained paused for a second, staring at the ball and then all around the courts.

"Do you miss it, being at The Home with everyone? The days we used to all be out here?" he asked.

Kim hated how stuck in the past he seemed to be at times.

"Truthfully, no. I didn't hate it there, I mean at least not at first, but when I had to come back.... I really didn't wanna be there. That's why I kept running away, why y'all could never find me."

"It's just kinda crazy you know," he bounced the ball back to her, "we're all out in the real world now. Like when we were all at The Home we were all safe, all the time. Now we're all spread out, a lot of us have moved out of the city and things just aren't like they used to be. When we were all close, like brothers and sisters."

Something about growing up in The Home that Blake always loved was that it felt like one big family. While many came and went there were always around twenty to thirty kids in The Home at a time. Being abandoned by his real parents, it felt good to feel loved and a part of something bigger than himself. He was the oldest around the time Kim, Joey, LuLu, and he were all there, so he happily took on the big brother role. He truly loved them all and always treated them like his little siblings. It was important to him that as they got older they all stayed in touch. This however didn't quite happen.

Whether work, school, significant others, or even children, just about everyone got into their own thing and communication between them all seemed to happen less and less.

Kim took a sixth shot and made it with ease. She walked forward and grabbed his arm.

"Hey, look at me," she said, turning his head towards her, "we're always gonna be brothers and sisters, all of us. Regardless of where any of us have gone or end up going, we're a family. We were all in there, together, going through the same stuff, all of us. Every day meant something. Do I miss it? Not really. I can't speak for everyone but I was going through some stuff losing my parents the way I did. I didn't necessarily wanna be there but that doesn't mean I didn't feel the love and certainly doesn't mean I didn't love you and everyone else in there with us."

A disappointed look still rested on his face. Kim knew there wasn't much she could do to change it; it was just how he was at times. Kim let his arm free and picked up the ball. She walked back to the three-point line and turned back towards him.

"For a while, y'all were the only family I had, and I probably never said it enough but I loved all of y'all. I was unhappy because of the hand I was dealt, but y'all were always there for me. Especially you. You were and still are the best big brother any of us could've ever asked for and it's great you're passing that same love onto them now," she said motioning over her shoulder to the younger kids.

His mood still unwavered, she took one last shot that passed smoothly through the net. She pulled her chain back out from her shirt and slightly shrugged in his direction.

"Call me if you need me OK.... take it easy," she said as she walked off the court.

~

Kim laid down in her bed and closed her eyes. She had felt slightly guilty all day for not being able to cheer Blake up earlier but she knew he would be OK; he just wanted a family. She couldn't fault him for that. They had all promised they would stay in contact, look out for each other, and remain close. He was really the only one who held up that promise.

She knew she could contact Blake at any time and LuLu was just next door, but that was it as far as anyone else from The Home went, all the others had disappeared. Then there was Joey, who she still currently needed answers from.

She quickly rolled over and pulled her cell phone off her nightstand but froze before even unlocking it, remembering they hadn't traded numbers, she had only given him hers.

She rested her phone back on her nightstand, rolled over, and forced herself to sleep.

~

Kim slowly stomped downstairs the next morning, again working on being at least fifteen minutes late for work. The ability to care was gone. She was prepared to be fired.

As she stepped down from the staircase her foot landed on something a lot higher than the floor. She lost her balance and stumbled forward catching herself on the wall. She looked back and saw Cindy's backpack sitting at the bottom of the stairs.

"Cin!" she yelled upstairs.

She grunted, aggravated, as she grabbed the backpack and walked it over to the kitchen.

"Stop leavin your bag at the bottom of the stairs!"

She hung the backpack on the back of one of the kitchen chairs when she saw a piece of paper drop out of it onto the floor. She bent down to pick it up and saw it was actually a couple pieces stapled together. All the papers were full of handwritten paragraphs that she immediately recognized as Cindy's handwriting. She began reading it, noticing it seemed to be about growing up in a foster home and read as a speech.

She walked upstairs with the papers in hand and barged into Cindy's room.

"Cin, what's this?" she asked, holding the papers up.

She was still half asleep as she rolled over and squinted at the papers. Her eyes widened a bit when she realized what it was.

"My speech for today..." she said.

"You're giving a speech today?" she asked.

"Yeah," Cindy yawned, "gotta read it in front of the school today."

"What? Are parents allowed to come?" Kim asked.

"Yeah.... they don't care who shows up."

"Why didn't you tell me?"

Cindy sat up in her bed.

"It's an early morning assembly. I knew you'd be at work. You're always so busy and when you get home you're usually too tired to do anything but cook and then you just go straight to bed. Honestly, I didn't think you'd really be that interested."

Her words hurt Kim's heart, mostly because she knew she was right, or as right as she could be. She was always doing something, always busy with something, and when she wasn't and was home, she was either sleeping or pretending to be asleep to soon sneak out. She did make it seem like she didn't have time for her. But where she was wrong was saying she wasn't interested.

She loved her as if she were her own and relished the thought of hearing her deliver a speech. It was something she felt as a parent she should be there for as she remembered her foster parents being there for her in similar instances. She felt awful that Cindy believed that she wouldn't care.

"Cin," Kim said, sitting on her bed, "anything that goes on with you, anything you do, I wanna be there. Doesn't matter how big or small. I know I haven't always in the past, but things are changing…. or *have changed*. Long story short I'm gonna have a lot more time now."

She noticed Cindy's eyes open wider as she said this.

"So when stuff like this comes up," she held up the papers again, "I wanna know about it cause I'm gonna do my best to be there."

"Mom, did you get fired?"

Kim rolled her eyes at her response.

"No…. well…. no, just please, let me know about things OK?"

"…. alright," she said.

"When is this?" Kim asked, holding up the papers.

"First period, in like an hour and a half,"

"Tell you what, I'll drive you to school today."

"Ummm…. what about work?" Cindy asked.

"They won't miss me if I'm a little late," she

assured her.

~

Kim entered the small auditorium of Cindy's school. The assembly had just started. Cindy's principal, the man she had spoken to last week, was at the podium thanking everyone for attending. The place was packed full of students and their parents supporting them. Kim began to feel guilty, wondering just how many of these moments she had already missed.

She pushed through a crowd and stood in the far back so she could see the entire stage. Cindy had told her on the ride there that she would be going first and that her speech wasn't too long. She also told her that there was no real topic for the assignment. Her teacher gave them the option to write about anything they wanted. This made Cindy's choice all the more interesting to her. As the principal wrapped up his introduction, he introduced Cindy to the auditorium. As she walked on stage with her papers in hand the crowd clapped welcoming her.

She stood behind the podium which she was barely able to see over, took a deep breath, and began reading.

"From the time I was three years old to when I was ten, I grew up in a foster home. It was hard to say the least. While young, I wasn't even aware of the situation I was in. I knew no better so I believed this was just how children lived. Growing older I realized this was not the case. Some children are lucky enough to have both parents in their lives, some fortunate enough to at least have one. Then there's kids like me."

The last line hit Kim hard, it was so relatable. This was part of the reason she had decided she wanted to adopt. She knew what the feelings growing up in a foster home did to a child and wanted to try to make a difference in at least one kid's life if she could.

"Never really having known the people who brought me into this world, not even being able to remember what they look like, a lot of things stuck with me, picked at me every day. However, the one that truly bothered me the most, and still to this day does at times, is the question of why? Why did I have to grow up in foster care? Whether it's unknown or whether whoever knew just thought it as best not to tell me, why did my parents leave me there? Did they leave me there? Or were they inept, unable, or just unwilling?"

Kim bit her lip in shame, she knew the answer.

"When you grow up the way I did the thoughts of what could've been weigh on you. Did they love each other? Did they love me? Were they nice people? Do I have any aunts or uncles? Any brothers or sisters? If I do, where are they? Where is my family? These are the questions I used to ask, but then I realized blood isn't what makes you family, love is."

Kim began to smile a little.

"I know plenty of people I grew up in foster care with I call my brothers and sisters, plenty of people in my life now that I call aunts and uncles. None of them share my blood. They all have one thing in common though, they love me, and love is all it takes to be family. I didn't learn this myself. Many friends, mentors, and loved ones helped me get to where I am now and I know I don't do a good enough job thanking them for all their help over the years. It'd be impossible to name them all but they know who they are and to them I say thank you so much. However, there is one person who I absolutely must mention and thank apart from the rest. The person who helped me the most in coming to these realizations of family and love by showing me so much love over the years; the woman I met at the age of nine, who would a year later adopt me as her own, my mom."

She made eye contact with Kim as she spoke the final words of her speech.

"Thank you, for everything. Everything you've taught me, showed me, given me, and done for me. Everything. I didn't truly know the meaning of family until I met you mom."

She took her eyes off Kim and scanned the audience and thanked them as well with a nod.

She stepped down and walked until she disappeared behind the stage curtains as the audience erupted into applause.

Kim pushed her back against the wall as she fought back tears. Another moment in which Cindy's own actions confirmed that Kim was not the complete failure of a parent she believed herself to be. She needed to go but she had to see her first. She shuffled through the still cheering crowd all the way to the stage and jumped up quickly disappearing behind the curtains.

Cindy spotted her first, "Mom?"

Kim fell down on her knees and embraced her tightly. Tears began to fall which she discreetly rubbed off on Cindy's jacket.

"I love you kid, I promise I won't miss another one," she cried.

"M-Mom.... get up," she moaned through her teeth, "people are staring."

Kim felt a tap on her shoulder. "Excuse me ma'am, we can't have you back here." Cindy's principal said.

Kim quickly stood up wiping her eyes.

"I-I'm sorry. I'm about to leave. I just needed to see her before I left."

She turned to Cindy and smiled. She grabbed her cheeks and shook them.

"I love you so much, tell your teacher I want that," she said, pointing to the papers, "it's going on the fridge."

"Oh god..." Cindy mumbled, "OK Mom, love you too."

As much as she tried to play it off in front of others, Cindy loved her and was thrilled her speech had moved her, and even happier she was able to see her deliver it.

When Kim got to her car she took a moment to just breathe and be thankful. It was both refreshing and a relief to know she was passing on something meaningful to Cindy. As the legal guardian of a child, she saw plenty of tough days. But moments like watching Cindy deliver her speech on stage made it all worth it. It was what she did it all for.

~

Kim speed walked to her desk to find a yellow piece of paper taped to the front of her computer screen. It was a write up. She sighed, crumpled the paper up, and tossed it into the trash.

"That's for not coming back yesterday. Boss doesn't even know you were late today," William said, standing behind her.

Kim cursed under her breath.

"What happened yesterday?" he asked.

"I told you I probably wasn't coming back."

"I thought you were joking,"

"Why? It's not the first time, why does it even matter?"

"OK, well what happened this morning?"

"Why?"

"Kim, they're gonna fire you," he pleaded.

"Yeah, why haven't they already? At this point I should be dead to them."

"Because we keep covering for you..."

"Stop! God! I told you to stop! I don't need you to cover for me, let whatever happens happen!" she growled.

Her tone was so aggressive William shrank before her. Kim realized what she had done and was disappointed in herself yelling at someone who was just trying to help her.

"Listen," she sat down with a now much cooler tone, "I'm sorry. I appreciate what you and Max are trying to do and have done but you gotta let me sink or swim on my own. Don't worry about me. I promise I can take care of myself."

He put his hands up slightly as if to surrender and nodded.

"Alright," he said.

"And for the record there was an excuse this morning, Cindy had an assembly at school. She had a speech she read out loud. I wanted to be there for her."

"You couldn't have called that in?"

"As many days as I've missed, calling and asking for even a morning off they'd probably have just laughed at me."

~

Kim sat at the kitchen table with a glass of tea, watching as Cindy finished up the dishes. She had pinned the essay to the fridge under a magnet and couldn't help but smile every time she looked over in its direction.

"Alright, finished. I'm gonna..."

Cindy stopped as she caught a glimpse of Kim's exaggerated smile.

"What?" Cindy asked.

Kim eyed in the direction of the papers and Cindy threw her head back in disgust.

"I knew I shouldn't have told you anything." she mumbled, "I'm going to bed."

"Wait wait wait," Kim said jumping up, "what made you write about that?"

"My teacher just said pick something, anything you care to write about. Off the top of my head it was something I knew that I knew well."

"You OK with everything though?" she asked, resting her hand on her head.

"Yeah I'm fine."

"Promise?"

"Promise."

"Alright, goodnight kid," she smiled, as she pushed her off to bed.

After she made it up the stairs and out of sight, Kim walked over to the refrigerator and looked at the papers. She lifted the first two up and read only the bottom of the last.

The last line on it read, *"It'd be impossible to name them all but they know who they are and to them I say thank you so much."*

No mention of Kim in the written draft she had read from. She had spit out the last few lines off the top of her head as she stared at Kim in the auditorium. This made her smile even bigger.

"Mom! Your phone's buzzing!" Cindy called from upstairs.

Confused Kim looked over to the counter where her cell phone was quietly resting. She stared at it for a few seconds longer until it hit her. She ran upstairs thanking Cindy from the hallway as she passed by her room. She opened her bedroom door and saw the small flip phone buzzing on her dresser. She just stared at it, letting it ring until it stopped. She then picked it up and read the small box of text on the front of the phone.

"1 new message, 1 missed call," it read.

She opened the phone and saw they were both from the same unstored number, because the phone had no stored numbers in it. It couldn't, it was too risky. But she knew who it was. Very few people had the phone's number. Only a select few she worked with, or use to work with rather. It was only to be used in emergencies two or three times and destroyed after.

"Hey, you ok?" the text read.

She kicked herself for being so careless again leaving the phone out in the open. She ran downstairs, out the door, and threw the phone in the garbage can to be emptied in the morning. As she got back into the house she remembered the coat closet and what was inside of it.

She slung one of the bags over her shoulder, put one under her arm, and one under the other. She kicked the door closed with her foot and tip toed upstairs past Cindy's room and into her own.

~

Joy City had a mood that woke up with it every single day. It didn't take long to notice it. This was probably because everyone inside the city knew what was in it, and what it had to offer, which wasn't much.

Kim found herself often staring out windows just watching things happen outside. In broad daylight she had seen fights, killings, crimes of all sorts, because that's what Joy City was; a haven for wrong doing. Some loved it, that's why they came to the city. Some, like Kim, were born into it, and hated it, longing for a way out.

"Kim?!"

Her attention whipped from the window to LuLu in front of her.

"You eatin today?" she asked her.

LuLu had picked her up from work for lunch and was offering to pay as Kim had fallen into a state of daydream.

"Just.... just some tea.... I'll pay you back tonight," she said, rubbing her eyes.

"Don't worry I got it, are you OK?"

Kim could only sigh in response.

"Work still eatin at you?" LuLu asked.

"Work is.... work is..." she shook her head unable to even finish her sentence.

"You still thinkin about quittin?"

"They'll fire me before I get a chance to quit," Kim told her.

"What?"

"I haven't necessarily been on my best behavior," she shrugged.

"What do you mean?"

"A lot has come up and I've missed a lot of hours."

A worried expression came across LuLu's face.

"So what happens if you lose this job, whether you quit or get fired?" she asked.

"I told you I got a plan. I'll be fine," Kim said.

LuLu cut her eyes at her.

"You know something..." LuLu said.

"I know what?" Kim asked.

"I don't know but you're way too calm about all this. You know something you're not telling me. Probably already got a new job lined up and you're just having me worry about you."

"Lu, I already told you not to worry. Just trust me, I'll be fine. Cindy will be fine, we'll be fine."

It was obvious she didn't believe her but she knew trying to pull something out of Kim was a lost cause.

"Alright, so how's Cindy anyway?"

Kim shivered as if remembering something traumatic.

"Actually, she had an assembly where she read an essay she wrote out loud at school."

"Really? How'd she say she did?"

"She did great. Actually I didn't even know she was such a good writer and she's a really good public speaker too."

"Wait, you went?"

"Barely. She didn't tell me about it because she thought I'd be too busy or wouldn't care and I just..."

"Awww.... Kim..."

"Lu, tell me the truth, am I terrible at this parenting thing?"

"No, don't say that. You're busy, making sure she's taken care of. You can't be a bad parent for that."

"I just don't feel like I give her the time she deserves you know."

"You can change that."

Kim sat back in her seat and looked up at the ceiling for a few seconds.

"I talk to her all the time Kim, she's happy. She's told me that. You know I wouldn't lie to you."

Kim nodded.

"Her speech was about The Home. She talked about the time she spent there, what she thought about her parents, and what family was to her. What really stuck out though was how much of myself I see in that girl, I think that's why I fell in love with her so quick. The things that she wondered, the questions she had about her parents, literally all the same things I thought about back then and still do now."

"Like what?" LuLu asked.

"The what-ifs. What if I wouldn't have been separated from my birth parents? What if they were still here, would my life be in better shape? Where even are they? Are they even alive? What if my foster parents hadn't been murdered, what if they were still here? Would I still be that happy privileged little spirit I was back in high school?"

LuLu made deep eye contact with her.

"Of course things would be different but you can't look at all that. It's in the past. You gotta keep your focus on what you have now, where you're at now. Don't doubt yourself."

Kim wanted so badly to tell her that her advice was way too broad. She wanted to tell her what she was saying wasn't helping but she didn't have the heart. LuLu was just another person trying her best to help her, she wouldn't be rude.

"Thanks," she said instead.

"Just tea?" LuLu asked, pointing at her.

"Yeah."

Lulu waved down the waitress as Kim dropped her head and fell deeper into her thoughts.

~

As Kim laid herself down to rest for the night, she continued to overwork her brain. Overthinking every little thing from every angle. From Cindy, to the conversation she'd had with Blake, to the one she'd had with LuLu, to work, and even The Pool, especially The Pool. She couldn't help but wonder about them, how things were going. Aside from the text the night before, she hadn't heard from any of them in about five days. It was a first. She had never gone that long without seeing or at least hearing from one of them. As happy as she believed she would be being free, she was actually quite uncomfortable with such a sudden change.

She shook her head in disbelief. After finally receiving what she had begged for for months, freedom from The Pool, there she was, giving more focus to it. *Go to sleep Kim* she thought as she pulled her head under her covers.

~

"We're so proud of you," a voice cheered from behind Kim.

158

She turned around from her desk and saw William and Max standing over her.

"You were on time today and you're still here after lunch," William added.

Kim cut her eyes at them both and turned back around.

"Yeah well the day's still young, don't tempt me," she snarled.

Max sat down at his desk and nudged Kim with his shoulder.

"You can make it."

"Please don't touch me," she breathed.

William sat down on the other side of her.

"Don't be like that," he said, pushing his shoulder against hers as well, "you know you love us."

Kim, now squished between them both, was slowly losing her patience.

"You know.... I could kill you both right now?" she said.

"But you wouldn't," William smiled.

Kim was opening her mouth to say something when her cell phone buzzed in her pocket. She opened her arms aggressively pushing them both away from her.

She pulled the phone out and saw a text from an unknown number.

It read, "Hey it's Joey, can you hang out tonight?"

She was both relieved and surprised to see his name.

She quickly texted him back, "I'll be off in a

few hours, I'll call you. Where are you at?"

She had so many questions for him. Where was he, whose phone was he using, what was he doing at the club last Friday?

~

"There's thirty dollars in the bottom drawer of the dresser, get whatever you want delivered," Kim said through the phone.

"Alright..." Cindy replied.

"But don't spend it all," she said firmly.

"Why would I buy thirty dollars' worth of food?"

"Because you eat like a thirty year old man."

Cindy sucked her teeth through the phone.

"Yeah alright, love you, bye."

"Love you too."

Kim was sitting in her car outside a local bar where she had agreed to meet Joey after she got off work.

She stepped out of the car into the cold night. She pulled the hood of her jacket up over her head and walked up to the entrance.

"Munchies" the sign above the small building read.

She walked inside to see the place wasn't too crowded. The environment smelled of everything synonymous with a bar, she hated it but would tolerate it for the answers she needed. She scanned around and eventually found him with his back to her sitting at the bar alone. She recognized him quickly from a camouflage hoodie he'd had since they were teenagers. She walked up behind him placing a hand on his back.

"Hey, what's up, how are you?" she asked.

His eyes were mildly bloodshot, there were bags under them. He looked exhausted. He had a drink in his hand that was already half empty.

"Hey," he said, his tone was dull.

"Glad you texted me, I've been worried about you," she said pulling her hood down.

He took a sip of his drink and looked at her with a plain stare.

"Told you not to worry, I'm fine," he said.

Normally she would argue but his tone seemed a bit more aggressive than usual. She assumed whatever he was drinking had already started to affect him.

"OK.... well, what's up? You said you were staying with a friend, is that whose number you texted from?"

"Yeah," he took another larger sip, "friend of the family."

"Well, glad you're safe. Glad you found a place to stay."

He didn't respond. An awkward silence came in between them as he spun the remainder of his drink in his glass. She found it odd he invited her but she seemed to be the one carrying the conversation.

"So, did you hear about that mess that happened at the club last week?"

Like ripping off a band-aid, she had to ask. It was the one answer she needed from him the most.

She had hoped to ease it into their conversation a little better but the prolonged silence called for something.

"Heard about it, hmph…. Joy City," he said as he finished off his drink.

"Yeah…" Kim whispered.

Another awkward silence came in between them, this one lasting longer than the first. She wanted to press more but the nonchalant way he had answered her first question made her rethink dragging the topic out any longer. Kim sat quietly while he continued swirling his drink in his glass.

"Joey, are you OK?" she asked cautiously, "I'm guessing you asked me to meet you here for more than just for us to sit?"

He pushed the glass away from him and pressed both his hands down on the bar. He stood up and looked at her with his eyes cut low.

"Yeah, let me show you something," he said, making for the exit.

Kim looked around confused. She got up, pulled her hood back over her head and followed him outside. He walked over to an old beat up blue car.

"Is this yours," she asked.

"For right now," he said.

His voice was as cold as the air.

He opened the door to the backseat on the driver side and leaned in. Kim stepped back and looked away trying not to appear too nosey. She looked up and down the street in front of them. She watched the cars passing by, the traffic lights flashing, and a few people walking down the sidewalks. She had turned away from Joey and began staring at a building a ways away from them. She keyed in on something on top of it. She looked, focusing until she made out the figure of a person. It looked like a man, standing completely still. He appeared to be watching them.

"Hey.... you see that person up there?" she asked.

She turned back around to face him and stared down the barrel of a pistol. She leaned back just as he fired, dodging the shot.

"Joey?!" she cried horrified, as she stared into his lifeless eyes.

A throwing blade suddenly hit the ground just inches from Kim's foot. The sound grabbed both their attention. They both looked in the direction of where Kim had seen the figure standing on the roof; it was gone.

Kim quickly looked back at Joey and slapped the gun from his hand. She cowered back before breaking away into a full sprint in the opposite direction. She ran down the street, rounded the corner and dipped into an alley. She pressed her back against a brick wall and began gasping attempting to catch her breath. She was torn, juggling a mix of fear and confusion. Her mind was racing, she couldn't wrap her head around what had just happened.

Suddenly a black hooded figure dropped down right in front of her. She shrieked and threw a punch that was caught.

"Hey hey hey, chill it's me!" a familiar voice said.

The figure pulled down the hood and mask covering their face; It was Aaliyah. Kim was completely thrown.

"W-what are you doing here?" she asked her.

"What are *you* doing here?" Aaliyah returned her question.

The sound of a gunshot echoed through the alley and Aaliyah went down with a loud grunt grabbing at her leg. Kim looked down to where the alley opened into the street and saw Joey with his arm extended. Before he was able to take another shot his hand was hit by another throwing blade that caused him to drop the pistol he was holding. Another figure in black dropped from a fire escape. Kim recognized it as the one she had seen watching them just before Joey had tried to shoot her. Joey broke to the left holding his hand until he was out of Kim's sight. Kim's heart was beating out of her chest; she was completely lost.

She crumbled to the ground checking on Aaliyah. She had been hit in the leg and was losing blood. The figure that had dropped down from the fire escape ran up, removing their hood and mask as well; It was Pedro. He ran over to them and knelt down.

"W-what just happened?!" Kim asked in a panic.

"A payday just got away that's what happened?!"

"What?!"

"Uhhh…. can y'all talk about this later, there's a hole in my leg," Aaliyah groaned.

"Charlotte's on contract tonight. Get her to the hospital as fast as you can, I gotta catch him," Pedro told her before running off.

"Wait..." Kim begged.

"Go now!" he yelled over his shoulder.

She looked down at Aaliyah and began to panic, still unsure of what she had just witnessed. She took her jacket off and wrapped it around her leg covering the wound. She pulled her to the side of a dumpster and propped her up against it.

"Look at me," Kim said to her, "keep breathing, don't try to move. I'm gonna run and get my car and come back to get you."

Aaliyah nodded as she winced in pain. Kim tucked her chain and took off into a mad sprint back the way she came.

Chapter 7

Helena II

"I just wanted to let you know, so don't wait up for me. I'll be home pretty late tonight, just.... catching up with an old friend," Kim said.

"Alright," Cindy yawned on the other end of the phone.

"Did you get yourself something to eat?"

"Yeah, I'm good, probably gonna head to bed soon."

Kim saw Pedro step out the elevator into the waiting room of the hospital where she had brought Aaliyah.

"OK Cin, I gotta go. Call me if you need anything, bye," she quickly rushed off the line.

She stood up as Pedro immediately made a beeline for her.

"Is she OK?" he asked.

"She's fine. They stopped the bleeding and got the bullet out, she's just resting."

Pedro let out a sigh of relief.

"What happened?" Kim asked him.

"I was gonna ask you the same question. Why were you with that guy?"

"That's my foster brother Joey."

"Your foster brother? I'm sorry, maybe I was trippin but you saw him pull a gun on you too right?"

"I'm just as confused as you are about it. What were y'all doin there though?"

"That was the guy, the target with the six-figures on his head that I told you about," he whispered.

"Joey?!" she sighed, as she buried her face in her hands and dropped back down into the chair.

She couldn't believe it. Someone she had loved like a brother had a price on his head.

"Kim, you weren't protecting him were you?"

"No? I never looked at the target's picture on those papers, I had no clue he was who y'all were after. He invited me out for a drink and…. well you saw what happened."

"Why'd you run from him? You've had more than enough training, you could've easily killed him right there."

"Pedro, he's my brother. We grew up with each other, we shared a bed together some nights," she said, as tears began to roll down her cheeks, "I was so shocked, things were happening so fast. My first thought wasn't to kill, it was why is this person I love trying to hurt me?"

"He must've found out, must've knew we were coming, probably thought you were on him?"

Kim was squeezing her head between her hands, clinching her teeth, sniffling as she fought her tears.

"I didn't catch him Kim."

She lifted her head up.

"He got somewhere where there were too many eyes. He got away but now he knows we're coming for sure," he added.

She released another distressed sigh.

"God Joey.... what'd you get yourself into," she whispered aloud.

Her voice was trembling.

"Will she be OK here by herself?" Pedro asked, thumbing towards the room Aaliyah was in.

"Yeah, they're gonna keep her overnight anyway."

"Then we'll come back in the morning."

"Where are you going?"

"*We*," he stressed, "are going to the pool hall. We gotta talk to Terrance."

As soon as the words left his mouth, she began dreading it.

"Why do *I* need to be there?"

"Really Kim?" he asked with a disgusted glare.

Rarely had she seen him so serious. She knew if she didn't go now, Terrance would eventually come looking for her, asking questions and demanding answers. They stared at each other intensely for a moment. Tears rested in Kim's eyes as impatience rested in Pedro's.

"After you," he said motioning her towards the elevator.

He knew he had her. He knew she knew that she needed to go. She dried her eyes, stood, and walked past him towards the elevator without a word. He followed closely behind her.

~

Kim and Pedro walked up to the back entrance of the pool hall. Pedro stopped just before opening the door and turned to Kim.

"Let me do the talkin OK? He knows things went south but I didn't tell him you were there. I'll try to keep him off you," he said.

Kim simply shrugged. Pedro opened the door and they stepped inside. She noticed nothing had changed in the week or so she had been absent, it was the same old place.

"Kim?"

Both Kim and Pedro's focus shifted to their left to see Charlotte sitting in a chair. She looked surprised to see them, or Kim rather. She, like everyone else, probably assumed Kim's last time being inside the pool hall was her final.

Charlotte was unpacking a small bag. Kim assumed she had just returned from the contract Pedro had mentioned earlier.

The sound of a chair scooting across a wooden floor came from the back room. Terrance poked his head out and his eyes grew wide when he saw Kim. He looked her up and down as she did him. The moment was just as intense as it had been the night of the club incident. Terrance's expression suddenly shifted from surprised, to annoyed, and what looked to be heading towards angry.

"Look..." he snarled stepping one foot out the door.

Charlotte quickly jumped up from her seat and stood in front of him. Pedro stepped forward as well as Kim remained where she stood.

"Hey chill, we're not here for you two to butt heads right now," Pedro said, "we got more important things to work out."

Terrance continued to mean mug Kim as she dismissed his stares completely.

"How's Aaliyah?" Charlotte asked.

"She's fine, she's just resting," Pedro told her.

"What happened?" Terrance demanded, "Should've been an easy kill."

"It was looking that way but then..." he trailed off and looked in Kim's direction.

Terrance rolled his eyes and shook his head.

"I should've known..." he whispered.

"You know what..." Kim said, stepping forward.

Pedro grabbed her and pushed her back.

"Stop, can you two please just..." he looked towards Terrance, "listen, here's what happened. We tracked him from the location we got the other night to the bar. He went inside and we waited for him to come out. When he came out, he wasn't alone."

Kim and Terrance made eye contact when he said this. Pedro then turned to Kim as well.

"You had your hood up. We didn't know it was you until you ran into the alley," he told her.

Terrance pushed Charlotte aside and stepped forward.

"Why were you there?" he asked Kim.

She stared at him blankly contemplating being difficult just for the sake of it. She knew what he was thinking and she was furious at him for it. She wanted so badly to spite him in the moment but decided it would do nothing but complicate and drag the situation out longer.

"Joey's my foster brother, we grew up together. He asked me to meet him at the bar earlier today. I thought we were just gonna talk, catch up.... but he tried to kill me for some reason."

"And it didn't occur to you to kill him first?" Terrance asked.

"No, it didn't occur to me to kill my brother," she snapped back, "and I didn't know he was the target either, so when he pulled a gun on me, I didn't think anything. I was scared and confused."

"Does he know you have ties to us?"

"I would've thought not, but after tonight I really don't know."

"Then why would he try to kill you?"

"Your guess is as good as mine."

Terrance rolled his eyes and laughed a little.

"Why did you bring her here again?" he asked Pedro.

"God..." Kim scoffed under her breath.

"Because she can help us, she knows more about him than we do. He tried to kill her and the only thing we have to go off as to why, is maybe, somehow, he found out we were coming and decided to try to pick one of us off. That's an aware target that knows at least one of us by name and face. He opens

171

his mouth and we're all through. We need her right now."

Kim couldn't tell if he was just talking or if he believed anything he was saying. Regardless, she appreciated him for it. She often felt he was the only one who would ever stick up for her.

Terrance's eyes shifted between the three of them and eventually came to a close as he fell into thought. He palmed his forehead and began pacing back and forth a short distance.

"So? Plan? Anyone?" he asked.

"We could try the location we tailed him from tonight but I doubt he's headed back there. Any idea where he might be?" Pedro asked Kim.

"From what he told me he's homeless, living on the streets I guess. He said something about staying with a friend but I don't know who or where, or if that's even the truth. Where'd you tail him from tonight?"

"Third house off Craner," Pedro said.

"Craner Avenue?" Kim asked, "That's Colt 45 territory."

"That's where he came from, maybe he's affiliated?"

The thought worried her.

"You two get over there now," Terrance said eyeing Pedro and Charlotte, "I don't care who's there, how sloppy it is, if he's there, kill him."

Kim's stomach dropped. Terrance walked back into the back room without another word. Pedro looked at Kim who was visibly distressed. She dropped her head and stepped outside the pool hall slamming the door behind her.

"Hey, pack up we can leave in five. Let me talk to her real quick," he told Charlotte before following Kim out.

He lightly jogged to catch up to her, grabbed her, and spun her around to face him. He could see in her eyes she was both angry and hurt.

"Kim, I'm sorry," he said.

"What?" she asked, attempting to hide her watery eyes.

"Kim, we have to.... you know we have to..."

"Go then! I don't care!" she said, pushing him aside.

She couldn't hold them any longer, her tears began to fall. She was heartbroken, her own brother. She couldn't believe it, yet it fell right in line with every other sad unfortunate happening that made up her life.

~

Kim dragged herself from her car to her front door and sloppily unlocked it. She stepped inside and let the cold air hit her tear stained cheeks. The day had been cruel to her. She looked up at the ceiling and just wondered how. How she went from an innocent little girl living in a foster home, to where she was now, countless people's blood on her hands, having to run in fear for her life from her own brother. She wasn't one to allow fear to get to her but there was no help for it tonight. No matter how fast she attempted to run from her life's woes, they

173

always managed to catch her.

She had finally gotten her wish, to live like a normal person again, without the pressure and secrecy being in The Pool bound her to. But just as fast as she believed she had shed that part of her life; it had caught up to her again and was now swallowing up those she loved as well. This was her worst nightmare.

She began to get dizzy. She braced herself against the wall after nearly tipping over. Her head was pounding. The pain caused her to let out a disgruntled moan. She quickly stabled herself, wincing in pain as she thought of Cindy upstairs sleeping. She didn't want to wake her and risk the possibility of questions she wasn't prepared to answer.

She then heard the sound of glass clanking against the table coming from the kitchen. She turned the corner and saw Helena sitting at the table holding a glass of tea. She was a bit shocked to see her. She thought about it and realized she hadn't actually seen her in about a week. However, unlike times before, she didn't immediately think to throw her out, she was actually somewhat relieved to see her. She wasn't sure why, but for some reason she felt some comfort in her presence.

Helena had not looked up to acknowledge her. She just continued to sip her tea looking straight ahead.

"Hey," Kim breathed.

"Hey, sounded like you were having a rough time over there. I thought about helping, but, you know.... you told me to stay away from you so I figured that was none of my business," Helena said, before sipping her tea.

Kim stood still for a few seconds before speaking again. She wiped her eyes and rubbed her nose.

"Haven't seen you in a while where.... where've you been?" she asked her.

Helena finally turned and looked at her. Her eyes got big as if surprised by the question.

"Where have I been?" she asked, "You told me to stay away from you, right? You said you were sick of me didn't you?"

"Yeah..." Kim said.

Helena simply shrugged and continued to sip her tea. There was another glass resting on the table directly across from her.

"Mind if I..." Kim pointed to the other glass.

"It's your house," Helena said behind her glass.

Kim sat down and took a sip of tea. It was cold which initially made her cringe. She thought about mentioning it but decided not to, taking a few more sips instead.

She purposely avoided eye contact with her. She wouldn't dare look but she knew Helena was staring at her waiting for her to say something. She held out as long as she could, examining every appliance in the kitchen until there was simply nothing left to look at. She slowly turned her line of sight towards her and locked eyes with Helena, who wasn't even trying to be discreet with her staring. She was shooting a blank stare across the table, waiting.

"Good to see you again," Kim gave her half a smile.

The smile was genuine, but in her current state of emotion, she couldn't muster anything better than half of one. Helena laughed under her breath at this.

"Is it?" she teased, "Is it really? Because, correct me if I'm wrong but I remember you saying something to the extent of if you ever saw me again, you'd kill me?"

Kim couldn't find words to counter; she knew she deserved her verbal jabs for the way she had last spoken to her.

"I'm sorry," she said.

"You don't have to apologize, I don't hold grudges," she told her, as her usual smile slowly returned.

They both continued to drink. Kim, looking all around, would occasionally make eye contact with her, but always tried to quickly move to something immediately after to avoid her sweet but daunting stare. Kim couldn't understand why she wouldn't look away, why she wouldn't stop smiling. The tension between them was growing thicker and thicker by the second.

"I know you have something to say, your body language speaks for itself," Helena whispered.

Kim hadn't expected her to be able to read her body language. No one ever seemed to be able to, but much to her surprise, Helena seemed to see right through her.

"It's nothing you'll answer directly so why

bother?" she asked, cutting her eyes slightly.

"So, it's a question then?" Helena responded.

Kim had forgotten how cunning she was, how quickly she was able to think on her feet. Kim ignored her and took another sip of tea.

Helena waited, giving her a chance to speak, but nothing. Kim remained mute, and so Helena spoke instead.

"Tell you what, you're exhausted, mentally, physically, and emotionally, I can see it. You've been in hot water with both your jobs all this week, you're stressing over your ability to give your daughter the time she needs and deserves. Your brother, who I tried to warn you about a few times, but whatever, tried to murder you. One of your friends is in the hospital with a hole in her leg because of you, and now your other friends are on their way to murder your brother for a check. It's been a long week for you. So, I'll do you a favor, I'll make it even easier for you. Ask me anything, anything you wanna know and I'll tell you the truth. I'll tell you exactly what you wanna know, I swear, no dancing, no changing the subject, whatever you wanna know. But you have to ask it right now."

Kim's eyes opened wide at her knowledge of so many events she hadn't been around for. It gave her chills thinking she may have been secretly watching her the entire time each one was happening. What was even more unsettling was her offer to answer her questions as she hadn't really answered a question directly since they had met. Her sudden willingness to took her by surprise.

"Anything?" Kim asked.

"Anything at all, no dodges, no ducking."

Helena held a very confident cocky grin on her face. Her smile was soft and her eyes were slightly cut, she appeared extremely relaxed. Kim believed she knew something.

"Ummm…. I can't really think of anything off the top of my head…"

"Not buying it Kim," Helena interrupted her.

"I-I don't have a question," she proclaimed.

"Kim!"

Helena's voice boomed as she cut her off. Kim had never heard her speak so harshly before. Her smile had faded, she now had a serious look on her face that Kim wasn't used to seeing.

"Kim," her tone now more hushed, "I already know the questions, and you already know I know. I'm willing to tell you exactly what you want to know, but I'm not going to if you don't ask first."

If she was serious about answering Kim knew she would regret not asking the questions she did have, but she also wasn't so sure she wanted to know the answers to those questions. By her smile, Helena was oozing confidence in whatever it was she had to tell. She knew something Kim didn't and she knew Kim wanted to know badly. If she didn't ask now, she knew Helena would tease her with it until she begged her to talk. It wasn't worth pretending she was truly absent of wonder. She dropped her head and took a deep breath.

"Who are you…. how do you know me…. how do you know so much about me…. how are you always just around wherever I..."

"I'm your offset."

Her smile returned. She looked so satisfied, like she was happy for the opportunity to speak the word again. Kim raised her head up to face her.

"You said that already, but what does..."

"I'm an offset to your emotional disposition," she continued, "Your offset. I'm sure you've noticed you and I are polar opposites, that's no coincidence. I am the half of you that's no longer apart of you. You might've also noticed only you are able to see me, hear me, or speak to me..."

Kim had honestly never paid much attention to it but thinking about it, it was true. No one else had ever acknowledged her presence.

"...that's because, I'm not real."

Kim's heart skipped a beat. Her words caused her to cock her head sideways.

"When you became an assassin years ago you were told you were not allowed to feel anymore. Compassion became a liability in your life. You were told to think from that point on as a killer, not a mother, not a daughter, not even a human being, but a cold blooded killer. To do that, you had to cast away your emotions permanently. Any feeling that wasn't required for you to be able to put a bullet between someone's eyes or stick a knife into someone's gut had to be purged from your mind, body, and soul, to allow focus and concentration. Happiness, love, hope, remorse, just to name a few, all began to be stripped away from every part of you. This left you with the only feelings you needed to take a life, disgust, sadness, a bit of anger, and of course, a little insanity."

Helena's smile widened as she spoke the last word.

"Your line of work naturally drives you insane the more you do it. No matter how heartless or ruthless you believe you are, constantly seeing people die by your own hands will eventually have an effect on your mental. Your mind has become so twisted, so mentally sick from the things you've seen the past six years, it's beginning to die. You purged those emotions of happiness, love, hope, and everything else you didn't need to kill people out of your mind. But emotions can't just disappear. They have to go somewhere; they have to exist somewhere."

Kim was terrified by every word that passed over her lips, but she couldn't stop listening.

"And so," Helena continued, gesturing towards herself, "here they are."

Helena began biting her bottom lip as she laughed to herself a bit. Her smile turned almost villainous as she paused to do this.

"You're mentally ill Kim, broken actually, and upon casting away your emotions, your brain manifested them into a being that only you can see and hear."

Her laugh intensified; it was teetering on maniacal.

"That being, is me." she smiled, "Kim, I'm not real, I'm only real to you and that brain of yours that's suffocating inside the horrible reality that you've subjected it to."

Helena paused, giving Kim a chance to speak but she said nothing. She was frozen. Helena shrugged in her silence.

"Hope all this is making sense, are you following me?" she asked.

Kim had her hand over her mouth, unable to speak; she couldn't believe what she was hearing. Helena continued smiling as she waited for Kim to respond.

"So…. I'm dreaming?" Kim asked.

"Not quite, this is real," she said, waving an open hand in the air, "everything you're seeing right now is real, except for me."

Kim just stared at her in silence.

"I know it's pretty wild, but hey, this is your doing, you're the crazy one here not me." she paused and thought for a moment, "Well, I guess since I'm technically you, just all the emotions that you cast away manifested into a being, I guess I would be crazy too, or at least half of a crazy person? I don't know, I'm not mad about it honestly."

She found hilarity in the madness she was putting Kim through, bringing about uncontrollable laughter in between sips of her tea. Kim was so shaken she had to remind herself to breathe.

"How?" Kim asked, finally finding a word.

"How what?" Helena asked, taking another sip.

"How is that happening," she asked pointing, "how are you lifting that glass of tea and drinking it. How did you even make tea if you're not real? I mean, I'm real, right?"

She raised one finger as she finished off the

glass. She set it on the table and slid it over to her. Helena motioned her to look inside the glass, it was empty.

"I just finished that glass of tea, right?" Helena asked.

"Yeah," Kim nodded.

"Wrong, you did."

Kim was stuck again, unable to respond.

"Listen carefully, try to keep up OK? I am not real, we just established this, but that glass and the tea that was inside it are, so there's really no possible way I could've interacted with it, period. But you just saw me do it, crazy right? We've also just established that you're crazy. Well, here's what's happening. Seeing and committing murder on a regular basis has completely destroyed your mind to the point where it skips sometimes, think of it like a scratched CD. Sometimes your mind blanks and you miss things including your own actions, you black out basically, that's how sick your brain is. Part of my existence is your mind's attempt to make sense of those blanks you experience. I didn't make this tea, you did, about an hour before you left the house to meet Joey tonight, both glasses. You noticed the tea was cold right? That's because it's been sitting here for hours. Just like the tea we had last Friday morning was cold. You made and drank those glasses too."

Kim couldn't even blink, all she could do was listen.

"I didn't just drink that glass of tea, you drank it before you left. But your mind skipped that, it's trying to catch up. That's where I come in. I sit in front of you, drink it, and suddenly sense is made of there being an empty glass on the table in front of you that you don't remember drinking. I also didn't buy that coffee maker, or knock over that candy dish at the school, that was you too. But your mind told you it was me, your mind played out a scene in your head where I did those things, because your mind needed to catch up. And so, to make sense of why you were suddenly holding a coffee maker at the door or why there was suddenly a pile of broken glass on the floor in the office, your mind put me there and made those actions mine. But realistically neither of them could've been me, because well.... I'm not real. This is also why it was impossible for you to get a read on me last week. It's hard to really piece together a profile on someone that doesn't exist."

A knot had formed in Kim's stomach, she was struggling to breathe. A splitting headache had also come over her.

"Oh, and the headaches, sorry, those are kinda me too. Typically, when you get those your mind is skipping and or has skipped and is realizing it needs to catch up, fill in the blanks, which is why I usually show up following head pains."

A look of complete panic had overtaken Kim's once curious expression. The dizziness was returning, she was growing nauseous.

"Hey, I know it's a lot to swallow but don't pass out on me, remember I'm not real so I can't really help you if you hit the floor."

"I've been killing for six years, why show up now and not six years ago?" Kim asked.

183

"When you first started killing, it excited you, or maybe scared you. Either or, you were feeling something. It was something new you'd never done before and you believed you were doing the right thing, picking up where your parents left off. It was pumping adrenaline into you. But as of recent you've become numb to the act. You've killed so much it doesn't even provoke a feeling anymore, that anxiety, or whatever it was you once had has disappeared. That was the last emotion you lost that created me."

Kim was speechless.

"Careful, you leave your mouth open like that for too long something could fly in."

"How is this all a joke to you?" Kim asked in horror.

"I guess cause, I *am* the joke," she smiled, "and it's only funny because it's true."

Kim buried her face in her hands.

"Let it sink in for a while, you'll be alright."

"I-I need to go lay down," Kim said as she stood and began walking towards the stairs.

Helena closed her eyes with a smile on her face. She leaned back in her chair lifting the two front legs off the ground and placed her hands behind her head.

"Anymore questions before you go? My offer to answer anything only lasts for tonight so anything else you wanna know you better ask now."

Kim paused and just stared at her horrified. Her view of Helena had been confirmed and then promptly turned upside down. Her own mind had created a being that was now haunting her. And as unsettling and terrifying as it was to hear, Helena's smile never faded as she explained it all to her. Never once flinching as she told of her imaginary existence to a killer with a poisoned mind. Kim could accept that she was crazy but she was just coming to realize how truly insane Helena was. But Helena was her own creation and so she was not to blame for her own insanity, Kim was.

"You warned me about Joey that day he was here, how did you know? I've had years of training reading people and somehow I misread him, but you knew."

"Eh, chalk it up as a woman's intuition. On top of that, I'm pretty sure I got most of your common sense and deductive reasoning when we split," she smiled.

"They're gonna kill him tonight..." she sighed.

"I doubt it," she said nonchalantly.

"Doubt what?"

"They're not gonna kill him tonight."

"Why not?"

"Tonight's just not his night to die. Now I can't say what tomorrow or the next day holds but tonight, no, he'll live."

Kim crossed her arms over her chest and blew a gust of air from her mouth.

"Anything else?" Helena asked.

"Am I safe.... is Cindy safe with me?"

Helena stood up, walked over, and grabbed Kim's shoulders.

"Kim, we don't always think the same, obviously, but we are somewhat of the same mind, you could argue two halves of the same mind. We share plenty of thoughts and I know how much you love and care about her, you'd never hurt her right?"

Kim shook her head no.

"Then she's fine, you're fine. You heard that essay she wrote, she's got the greatest mom in the world. She's safe so long as you continue to do whatever you feel you need to do to keep her safe. Your mind may be a little broken but your heart's not, you'd never hurt anyone you cared about."

"But how can I be sure?"

"Because I just sat at that table and swore to you I'd tell you the truth. Trust me Kim. I know that's a lot easier said than done but just trust me, trust yourself."

As much as she wanted not to believe her, she couldn't think of a reason how or why she would compose such an extravagant lie. It made sense, her constant appearances, disappearances, her knowledge of her, everything.

"Get some rest, you've had a long day," Helena whispered, patting her shoulder, "I'll clean up down here."

Kim turned to head upstairs.

"I mean.... *you'll* clean up down here.... you know," Helena corrected herself laughing.

Kim paused as she came to the bottom of the stairs and watched as Helena picked up the glasses and begin washing them out in the sink. She was truly thrown.

She heard the glasses banging against each other and the sides of the sink, the water rushing from the tap, she couldn't believe it. It all looked so real, sounded so real, but none of it was. She began questioning everything she had seen and experienced since Helena walked into her life.

Chapter 8

Joey II

Kim jumped in her sleep at the sound of a knocking at her bedroom door. She quickly rolled herself out of bed and rushed to the door. She opened it to see Cindy eyeing her in a very peculiar way.

"Morning sweetheart, what's up?" Kim greeted her.

"Morning?" she questioned, "Morning's been passed, what happened to breakfast?"

Kim whipped her head around to the small clock on her wall.

"12:04" it read.

"Shoot," she whispered under her breath, "I'm sorry kid, I must've overslept."

"Nine is oversleeping for you, you're usually always up by then. I thought you were in here dead."

"Not quite," she whispered, "hey, boil me some water and preheat the oven. I'll be down in a minute."

Kim had gotten to bed extremely late after everything that had happened the night before.

Between dropping Aaliyah off at the hospital, stopping by the pool hall, speaking with Helena, and then the hours she laid in bed trying to wrap her head around everything, sleep didn't come easy.

She grabbed her cell phone off the nightstand and checked it. No new messages or missed calls. She wasn't exactly sure why she thought there would be or what a message might say even if there had been one. Truly she was hoping for a text from Joey explaining what he was thinking last night. But then the thought of someone within The Pool confirming a kill struck her. Or perhaps a direct apology from Pedro for committing the act? Suddenly Helena's words ran through her mind.

Tonight's just not his night to die...

Kim walked down the stairs but stopped as she got to the bottom. She looked around and saw nothing. The only thing she heard was the pot of water boiling on the stove and a voice or two coming from the TV in the living room. She stepped through the kitchen and onto the carpet of the living room where Cindy was lying across the couch.

She turned around to be spooked by Helena sitting with her feet up on the kitchen table.

"Morning gorgeous.... or afternoon I guess, how'd you sleep?" she smiled.

Kim walked up to the table and addressed her in a hushed voice.

"Did they kill him?" Kim asked her.

Helena appeared surprised by her question. Her eyes widened and her head jerked back slightly.

"Kim," she laughed, "I'm not the grim reaper, I

don't oversee death. I wasn't with them last night, I was here with you. How would I know?"

Kim released a displeased sigh. She pulled out a chair from the table and sat down.

"Last night you said..."

"I know what I said," she paused, "don't know if I'm right though."

Kim buried her face in her hands.

"That's something you're gonna have to ask them yourself," Helena added.

Kim angrily stood up from her chair and paced back and forth.

"Threw my burner phone out. Stupid," she growled at herself.

"Kim, I was joking. What would you even be asking for? If the answer is no, you gonna try to protect him? Try to get him out the city before they get to him? Mind you he tried to kill you last night."

"But what if the answer is yes?"

"Then it really doesn't matter," Helena shrugged.

A hard truth Kim wasn't prepared to accept. If they had killed him already, then there really was nothing more to ask or say.

"Cin!" Kim shouted from the kitchen, "Pancakes OK?"

A quick subject change spelled she had nothing else. No further argument or point to make. She knew Helena was right but felt no need to admit it.

"Waffles!" Cindy yelled back.

Kim looked at Helena who was lightly smirking at her. She shrugged and turned her head.

Kim continued to stare at her. While still a bit unsettled by her presence, something felt oddly comforting about her now. Especially having a better understanding of who and what she was. It all gave her a little more peace of mind. This was at least until she remembered that in a nutshell it all boiled down to her being insane and suffering from what were basically hallucinations.

"Get your feet off my table," she said turning towards the stove.

"Yes *mother*," Helena smiled, mocking her as she dropped them to the floor.

A knock came at the front door.

"It's open Lu!" she called over her shoulder.

"How'd you know it was me?" LuLu asked as she stepped inside.

"No one else visits me but you."

Helena scoffed at this, prompting Kim to side eye her.

"That's because you don't go out enough," LuLu said.

"Oh really? Last time I left the house you took me to a club where a shootout almost broke out."

LuLu rolled her eyes.

"Yeah yeah, blame me for everything," she said.

Cindy rounded the corner into the kitchen.

"Hey sweetheart," LuLu said pulling Cindy close to her and kissing the top of her head.

"Hey Aunt Lu," she smiled.

"Cin, go wash up, it's not gonna take long for these waffles to get done," Kim said.

She watched as she ran upstairs. Once she was completely out of sight her focus shifted to LuLu.

"I need a favor Lu."

"Uhhh.... OK?"

"I need you to take Cindy somewhere today."

"Where?" she asked.

"Anywhere, she just can't be in or near this house."

LuLu looked at her oddly.

"Kim, what's wrong?" she asked concerned.

"I just don't want her here today by herself and I'm gonna be gone for a while after we eat."

"But.... why?" she asked.

"Lu I really can't explain right now. Please, I just can't right now."

LuLu grabbed her hand and sat her down in the chair next to where Helena was sitting. She was watching their entire discussion with her usual look of merriment on her face.

"Kim, what's wrong?" she asked again, the look on her face told how worried she was, "You never explain things to me, like you're afraid of what I'll say or think or something. You do know you can tell me anything right?"

Kim loved her for trying, and had it been anything else other than what it was, she would have told her.

"I know..." Kim breathed.

"So why don't you?" Helena remarked under her breath.

Kim kicked her foot out hitting Helena's chair leg. It scooted across the floor loudly. LuLu turned to her side looking at the chair and then back at Kim.

"Sorry.... muscle spasm..." Kim said.

She jumped up from the chair and quickly moved past the subject.

"Please, I just really need her out the house while I'm gone. Please. It'll be great. She loves spending time with you."

She was trying to sell it as best as she could. Kim was extremely uneasy not knowing the status of Joey. If he was alive, he knew where she lived. She was worried he might come to her front door to finish what he couldn't the night before. She decided to go to the pool hall and ask for herself. Just to be safe, she decided she didn't want Cindy inside the house by herself.

"Alright," LuLu said.

"Thanks Lu, I owe you one," Kim said.

"You owe me like twelve, can you at least tell me something when you get back?"

"Sure, I really just gotta go see a co-worker of mine about something."

"Is that whose car is outside?" LuLu asked peeking out the window.

"What?" Kim asked, turning around slowly looking at her.

"There's an old blue car outside in the driveway," she said.

Kim rushed over shoving LuLu out the way. She looked outside and saw it was the old beat up car Joey had been driving last night. The windows were tinted too dark to see anybody inside. Her eyes grew wide.

"Oh god..." she whispered.

"What's wrong?" LuLu asked.

Kim jetted out the kitchen and raced halfway up the stairs just as Cindy rounded the corner. She froze in fear seeing Kim rushing towards her.

"Uhhh.... hey?" she said.

"Are you OK?" Kim asked.

"What? I was only up for a minute," she said.

Kim continued up the stairs blowing by her. She ran up and down the hallway in a panic checking all the rooms of the house.

Cindy hadn't moved, she was still staring at her confused. LuLu had moved from the kitchen to the bottom of the stairs.

"What is she doing?" she asked Cindy.

Cindy simply shrugged. Kim pushed past her, and down the stairs and then past LuLu. She made her way back to the kitchen and saw the car had started and was taking off down the street.

"No no no..." she groaned under her breath.

She grabbed her keys resting on the counter and ran to the coat closet. She quickly pulled out a pair of shoes, slipped them on, and jerked the front door open.

"Kim what's going..."

"Listen I gotta go. I need both of you to get away from this house as fast as possible."

"But..."

"Now!" she shouted, as she slammed the door shut behind her.

The car was gone by the time she got outside. She cursed under her breath. She then recalled the location Pedro mentioned the other day.

Third house off Craner...

She believed it was a long shot but it was all she had. She ran to the back of her car, ripped the license plate from the bumper, and frisbeed it into the bushes a few feet from her. She jumped in her car and sped off. She drove with purpose. She ran stop signs, red lights, exceeded every speed limit, and took every chance she shouldn't have to get there faster.

"Whoa speed racer, slow down before you get a ticket," Helena smiled from the backseat.

Kim rolled her eyes and scoffed at her.

"So Kim," Helena began as she climbed over the center console into the front seat, "what's the plan here? If that's him in that car and he's going where you think he is, don't you think he knows you're gonna follow him? Sounds like you're running straight into a trap here."

"I gotta talk to him," she said under her breath.

"OK.... and what if he's in more of a shoot first ask questions later type of mood?"

Kim ignored her question as she rounded the corner turning onto Craner Avenue. The street, the houses that lined both sides of it, and the neighborhoods that surrounded it were all run down. It easily read as gang territory.

Kim spotted his car quickly, third house just like Pedro had said. She pulled over to the opposite side and turned off her car.

Staring at the house she noticed the door to both the car that had taken off from her house and the door to the house it was parked in front of were left open.

"He's in there," she whispered aloud.

She opened the door and started to get out as Helena grabbed her by the arm.

"Kim? He left that door open for a reason. He knows you're tailing him, you're just gonna stomp right in there?"

"I don't even know that it's him in there," she said.

Helena looked at her dumbfounded.

"And that makes it better? Look where we are, you don't know what kind of ruthless killers might be waiting in that house."

"I'll take the risk. The chances of there being two murderers in the same house at one time are pretty low."

Helena, hearing her response, stared at her with both amazement and confusion.

"Wow…. I was right, I really did get all your common sense."

Kim jerked her arm from Helena's grip and stepped out the car.

"Hey, maybe you should at least call Pedro for backup?" Helena suggested, hanging out the passenger window.

"No!" she shouted over her shoulder.

"OK, well…. what if *I* was backup…"

"No!" she shouted again, continuing to walk towards the house.

Her pace slowed the closer she got to the house. Cigarette butts and crushed beer cans riddled the lawn in front of the house. She looked up and down the street, it was quiet. She found it odd for what she knew about the area.

Inching closer she saw what was left of the storm door was swinging open. To leave a door wide open in the middle of gang territory seemed reckless to her. Unless whoever was inside knew they wouldn't be bothered.

"Joey!" she called inside.

There was no answer. She stepped closer and called for him again.

"Joey! It's Kim, I saw you sitting outside! Joey?!"

There was still no answer. She gently pushed the screen door aside. It creaked loudly, eventually crashing against the side of the house. She peered inside to see the house was trashed.

"Joey! We gotta talk!" she called.

Her head now fully inside the house, she looked around what appeared to be the living room. Broken glass, trash, holes and cracks in the walls, furniture torn to pieces, it looked abandoned.

She pulled her head from inside and checked all around before stepping in. The stench inside was foul, so horrible she couldn't even place it.

"Joey?!" she called again.

She walked slowly across a sea of shattered glass and garbage. She saw a TV pulled off its stand lying flat on the floor, a recliner that had been tipped on its side with several chunks of its upholstery ripped out, and a book case tipped completely over. It looked like a tornado had hit the place.

As she looked around her eye caught a single photo lying face up on the floor still in its frame. It wasn't even cracked, it appeared to be the one piece spared in whatever destructive force hit the house. She knelt down and picked it up. There were three people in the photo. One of them a young Joey, younger than he was when they had met at Little Angels. Kim assumed the other two, an older male and female, were his parents. They looked so happy; Joey looked so happy. She remembered the first day she saw him at The Home. He had what appeared to be a permanent scowl on his face, but not in this photo. She couldn't recall a time ever seeing him so happy. She actually envied him for a moment. Moments and memories like it were what she never got to experience with her own birth parents. She couldn't help but feel a bit jealous.

Her cell phone then vibrated in her pocket. She pulled it out and saw a text from LuLu

"Hey what happened?" it read.

She looked at it and then back at the photo in her other hand shaking her head. The things she wished she could tell.

She froze as she heard a sound behind her, the shuffling of glass. She quickly turned around and saw Joey standing in the hallway opening with a gun pointed in her direction.

Before she could even think he shot and hit her in the shoulder. She dropped both her phone and the photo and collapsed to her knees. She grabbed her shoulder and let out a cry of pain. Tears began to fall at the same time. Joey hadn't budged, he was still holding the gun towards her but hadn't made another move. Her head was bowed, she was waiting to hear a second shot but it never came.

She picked her head up from the floor and made eye contact with him. He was just standing there watching as she cried writhing in pain with the blankest, coldest of stares on his face.

"Joey, what.... why.... why are you doing this? What did I do?" she asked, shaking in fear as tears rolled down her cheek.

He walked forward a few steps now pointing the gun at her head. She shut her eyes tight, and began to cry harder.

"Please just tell me why first!" she pleaded, "If you're gonna do this tell me why! What did I do?!"

Her eyes remained closed. She could only wait for his answer or her end. She could feel herself breaking down. She couldn't believe what was happening, her own brother. She waited and waited and waited, and then he spoke.

"The man who adopted you was a murderer."

Kim immediately stopped crying and opened her eyes.

"What?" she asked looking up at him.

"My dad was one of the original Colt 45s of Joy City, old as the name itself. He was one of the gang's leaders when the raids happened. The weight his name held in Joy City's streets was both a blessing and a curse. Powerful people make enemies easily, and he had plenty, one of them called for his head. Your father killed him."

Kim was speechless. She felt a pit deep in her

stomach.

"He ran in our house, unmasked, and gunned my dad down right in front of me, did my mom the same. Then he looked me in my eyes. He didn't say anything, but his stare haunted me for the rest of my life. I'll never forget it, then he just left. I was sent to The Home a week later."

Kim wasn't breathing, all she could do was stare at him with her mouth open.

"I heard whispers from everyone, family, friends, members of my dad's gang, they all said the same thing, assassination. I saw him with my own eyes and promised myself if I ever saw him again, I'd kill him myself, but I never got the chance.... retaliation. My dad's gang got to him first, and then you showed up at The Home shortly after. I had no clue back then, but that picture you showed me..."

He had recognized Kim's father from the photo above her refrigerator. It was why he had begun acting so strange after she showed it to him.

".... it all made sense then." he let out a small laugh, "My dad's gang took both sets of your parents from you. After what your dad did to me, to the 45s, I'd say that's appropriate."

Kim clinched her teeth hard. She was furious, a gang she had worked so close with the past six years responsible for the loss of all her family. She couldn't believe it.

"And now," Joey pushed the gun closer to her head, "you're all that's left. Didn't get to murder your father myself but killing his daughter will do just fine..."

"Joey no! Listen, I didn't know, please! We've both lost too much already! We're the only family we have left! Joey please, my arm, I'm losing blood!" she cried.

"We're not family, your father took the only family I had and if..."

He stopped ranting as a light vibrating sound distracted him. They both looked around searching for the source. Kim saw it first, her phone she had dropped when Joey shot her. It was ringing face down. Kim looked up at Joey still searching for the sound and acted before she even thought. She pulled her hair pick from her waistline and threw it at him. He let out a grunt as the blade stuck into his arm. He dropped the gun at his feet. Kim pushed herself up and rammed her shoulder into his chest. He stumbled back falling to the ground.

Kim rolled her shoulder a few times, picked up the gun he had dropped, and stomped towards him with a look of absolute disgust on her face. She let out a low growl as she stood over him.

He looked at her with eyes full of hate. He began smiling menacingly, slightly chuckling to himself. He nodded at her.

"Do it Kim.... do it!" he said.

She wiped the tears falling from her cheek as she snarled back at him.

"This is where it starts, the first kill. Once you get that taste of blood, you'll do it again, and eventually end up just like your dad, killing the innocent for a little change in your pocket."

He had no clue of Kim's tie to The Pool; she

doubted he even knew of its existence.

"Your dad's gang took everything from me," Kim huffed through gritted teeth.

"And your dad took everything from me," he responded.

Kim began to shake. She was beyond furious, far past hurt, and terribly confused. Had it been anyone else she wouldn't have thought twice about pulling the trigger. But regardless of everything, he was still her brother. She couldn't.

She cursed aloud, stomped her feet into a pile of glass, and began crying again. She couldn't do it, after everything, she couldn't even say she wanted to. She was already short on family; she wouldn't allow herself to be the reason she became even shorter. She turned away from him embarrassed prompting him to begin laughing at her.

"You care too much," he said gripping Kim's hair pick, "I should already be dead. I wanna be dead, and if you're not gonna do it..."

Kim turned to face him as he pulled the bladed pick out from his arm and quickly zipped it across his neck, killing himself. Kim gasped, cursing aloud. Her jaw dropped as she froze in fear. She couldn't believe what she had just seen. She was broken, it felt like her heart had been torn in two. She had seen so much worse in her years in The Pool but to stand over the lifeless body of someone she cared so dearly for was different. She felt her stomach begin to turn.

She picked up her phone and carefully reached over Joey's body to grab her pick. She wiped it off on her pants leg and stepped back taking one last look at him.

"I'm…. I'm sorry Joey..." she whimpered.

She kicked down the back door and ran through the backyard. She cut through a small patch of trees until she came out on the other side that opened into the road. She was twitching, becoming dizzy, her stomach felt empty. She couldn't recall a time feeling so horrid other than the day she was told her parents had been murdered. She sat down on the curb to catch her breath. She wiped a few tears from her eyes and released a few sighs of agony.

She unlocked her phone and viewed her missed notifications.

"1 missed call, Cindy"

"1 new message, Cindy"

She unlocked the phone and read the message.

"Are you ok?"

Kim dropped the phone on the pavement beneath her and let every tear she had left fall.

Chapter 9

Family

"This might sting some," Charlotte said.

She pushed a cloth over Kim's shoulder and began wrapping it in gauze. Kim exhaled hard through the pain.

"You'll be fine, just try not to move it too much." she added, "Make sure you come see me in a few days so I can clean and rebandage it too."

"Thanks," she grunted.

Kim, with a hole in her shoulder, had walked her way back to the pool hall. She decided to abandon her car to avoid being spotted leaving the house where they would soon find Joey's body.

She had cried the entire walk across town, holding her shoulder, asking herself why. She was more than hurt. Between witnessing her brother take his own life, learning the truth about her parents' murders and what led up to them, she was a mess, she felt mentally and emotionally wrecked.

As she stood to her feet Terrance stepped out of the back room and eyed her. After she had explained everything he simply walked to the back room in silence. They stared each other down for a few seconds. She hoped he would stay in the back room until after she left. She was expecting to be chewed out by him for again interfering with a contract she wasn't assigned to. She knew he wouldn't let her go without some words.

He began marching towards her. She sighed and rolled her eyes.

"Listen, I know..." she began.

She went silent as he tightly embraced her. The initial surprise made her entire body go tense. The last thing she had expected from him was a hug. For as long as she had known him, she could only remember one other time receiving a hug from him, the day of her foster parent's funeral. She eventually let her body rest and hugged him back.

As unexpected as it was, it felt good, and she needed a hug from him. He no longer felt like a stranger to her as he had the last two times she had seen him. He felt like family again.

Memories they shared together after her parent's deaths began rushing through her head. The times they would stay up past midnight watching movies together at his house whenever she ran away from The Home. The day he picked her up from the police station after she had been caught stealing a laptop from a department store. The car he bought her, the one her parents promised they would for her sixteenth birthday, and how she totaled it in a mere three days. Two weeks after her eighteenth birthday, when he sat her down and told her of The Pool and all her parents' secrets. Nearly two years later, the day he revealed the hidden blade within the hair pick her father had given her and she used it to confirm her first kill.

He pulled back holding onto her arms. She could see his eyes were red from crying.

"I'm sorry," he said, his deep voice trembling, "had I known it was them, we'd have never worked with them. I'd have killed them all a long time ago."

He was extremely bothered by the 45s being responsible for the death of his best friend and partner.

"What can be done?" she whispered.

"And your other folks.... I knew about the raids but I didn't know that's what separated you from them."

"All these years, we never really talked about it. It's fine, it's all in the past now."

He looked defeated. After Kim lost her foster parents, he swore to protect her and at that moment he believed he had failed.

"I-I don't know if I can do this anymore. As funny as it sounds, I've been doin it for six years, but today was really the first time it hit me that I'm not invincible. I could've died today. I don't know that I'm OK with that."

"I get it..." he whispered.

"I'mma go see my daughter," she breathed, turning away from him.

"Yeah.... that's good." he said, "Get some rest too.... love you Kim."

She turned back slightly and whispered over

her shoulder, "Love you too."

She passed Charlotte on her way to the door.

"See you later," Kim said to her.

"You better," she smiled, "be safe."

"Always," she said stepping outside.

She opened the door to see Pedro with a phone up to his ear.

"Ahhh.... here she is, right here," he said as he saw her.

He handed the phone to her. She put it up to her ear and spoke.

"Hello?"

"Hey! That hole in your arm sucks don't it?!" a friendly voice asked.

"Hey Aaliyah, how are you?" she asked, shaking her head at Pedro.

"Oh I'm great, heard you got shot! Not so fun is it?" she laughed.

She couldn't resist teasing her knowing she was fine.

"Yeah yeah, karma I guess," Kim said.

"P told me what you went through today though, real sorry about your folks and your brother," she said losing her playful tone.

"Yeah, it's not been my favorite day," she whispered.

"Keep your head up girl, you know we love you and we gotchu. Anything you need you know where to find us."

"Yeah, love you too, get well."

"You too."

Kim handed the phone back to Pedro.

"Me and Charlotte will be up there later today, we'll see you then."

"Cool," she said.

Pedro hung up the phone and then snapped it in half throwing it at his feet.

He looked back up at Kim and smiled.

"What's up?" he asked.

"A ride home would be great."

"Hold on, talk to me Kim. How you feelin?"

"How am I supposed to be feeling?" she asked, "I watched my brother kill himself today after he tried to kill me twice."

"OK OK, stupid question. What's next for you then? Do you know where you're goin from here?"

"I don't know, but right now I just really wanna go home. Tell my daughter I love her and apologize for being such a terrible parent..."

"No no no, not this song again. You're not a terrible parent, don't say that. You're trying, you're doing your best."

"What am I even gonna tell her about this?" she sighed looking at her bandaged shoulder.

"It's Joy City, you don't have to tell her anything. Gang war crossfire, that's it."

"I'm so tired of lying to her though," she said shaking her head.

"It's for her protection though."

"Yeah, I guess.... take me home? I really need to see her."

"One more thing," Pedro gestured towards the door behind them, "you done here?"

Kim paused for a moment, thinking. After

everything she had been through in just the morning alone, yes should have been the obvious answer but oddly enough, it wasn't.

"I can't answer that right now, I just need to see my daughter," she said.

Pedro shrugged and nodded. The two quietly walked the hidden path leading out to the road.

~

Kim woke up from what should have been a deep sleep. She rolled over and looked at her alarm clock.

"12:34" it read.

She tossed and turned but couldn't force herself back to sleep. She was surprised she had gotten any sleep at all. There was so much on her mind, she was amazed it hadn't just exploded yet.

Warm tea, her answer to everything. She crept down the hallway and then downstairs, careful not to wake Cindy. She tip toed into the kitchen and flicked on the lights. In the middle of the kitchen table was the framed photo of her foster parents down from where it normally rested on top of her fridge. She walked over and picked it up. She was so torn.

She had known for years now what they had done in their past. She had forgiven them for those sins and hoped they had forgiven her for committing the same ones. She stared at her father on the left side of the photo. Learning what he did to Joey's parents, right in front of him, she couldn't help but despise the act. She let her eyes drift over to the right side of the photo and looked at her mother. Kim knew she was involved with The Pool from its inception but she often wondered just how much. Was she also an assassin or was she just associated with it all through her father's involvement? She wondered if she knew about the murder of Joey's parents, and if so, did she approve? Did she scold him for being so careless and for committing such a heinous act in front of a child, did she even care at all? She found herself feeling disappointed in them both.

In her eyes, her foster parents' singular flaw was The Pool. They were amazing, loving, kind, and generous people, but they were also murderous assassins. She hated to blame them for what she ultimately said yes to herself but she knew had they not been a part of it the chances of her ending up in it would have been slim to none.

She walked over and placed the frame back on top of the fridge where it belonged.

"You know, they weren't bad people. They just did a few bad things. I think there's a difference."

The sudden spoken words made Kim cringe. She turned around to see Helena sitting at the table with a glass of tea in front of her and one sitting on the other side of her just as she had the night before.

"Yeah.... I guess," Kim mumbled.

"You seem down, what's up?"

"Down isn't the half of it."

"Sit, talk to me," Helena said behind her glass.

Kim took a seat in the chair across from her. She tilted her head to the side attempting to recall the entire day in a moment.

"I've been doing this for some years now. I've seen a lot, done a lot, but for the first time today I honestly feared for my life. I could've died."

"Could've," Helena repeated.

"I'm not comfortable with that..."

Helena chuckled to herself.

"Well Kim, most people don't necessarily run to embrace death."

"No, not that, I accepted the fact that I could die any day doing what I do a long time ago. My issue with it is if something happens to me, Cindy gets refostered, just like I was. I'd be putting her in the exact same situation my foster parents put me in years ago. Picked up just to end up going right back. I don't want her to have to go through that like I did."

"So don't die?" Helena suggested.

Kim shot her a disapproving glare.

"It was a joke Kim, it's called a joke. Just tryin to lighten the mood up a bit, you got it all sad and mopey in here," she smiled.

Kim fell back into her chair and let out a sigh. She shook her head at herself as she cursed under her breath.

"So, what are you gonna do? What's your plan, what are you gonna do to keep that from happening? You quittin?" Helena asked.

She thought for a second. She squinted her eyes and looked back at Helena shaking her head.

"Is it crazy to say no?" she edged out.

Helena shrugged drinking her tea.

"I just.... I don't think I can. Knowing Joy City, I doubt there will be much of an investigation, but as bad as Joey's suicide looks, if an investigation does happen, they're gonna find me all over the house. Terrance can pull some strings and keep me clean. I think I might need them for protection alone."

"Hmph.... nope, not buying it Kim," Helena said kicking her feet up on the table.

"What?"

"After all you've been through you don't think he'd understand if you decided to hang it up? You don't think he'd still protect you if you told him you were done? C'mon, what's the real reason you won't walk?"

Kim hated how intuitive she could be, how easily she saw through fibs. She wondered if that was how she herself came off to people. Or how she used to rather.

"I mean.... they're also family I guess?"

"You guess?" she dropped her feet back down and leaned over the table, "Kim, they love you, any one of them would take a bullet for you. One of them did a night ago. There's nothing to guess about, they've been your family for the better part of six years. Always been there for you, looked out for you, protected you, and you have to guess?"

She rested back down into the chair and shook her head.

"I'm disappointed in you K, you just lost one of the few family members you had left and now you're hesitating to call family the four people who have been there for you unconditionally for over half a decade? K, you and these people commit murder together and then break the bread that you make doing it with each other. That's not something friends do, that's a family business."

Kim knew she was right. If anyone was family it was those in The Pool, those she trusted with her life and deepest darkest secrets.

"You're right."

"I know I am, remember your common sense is in here somewhere," she said, pointing to herself.

"Can't walk out on them cause they never walked out on me."

"This is true, but how OK are you with this? At the end of the day, if you're tired of doing it and think it's jeopardizing your ability to be what you need to be for Cindy, don't force yourself to stay."

"Is it terrible that the thought of not doing it actually scares me? Like I wouldn't even know what I'd do with all the extra time."

"I'm just taking a shot in the dark here but, how bout be a mom? You know, the thing you were wanting to quit for in the first place?"

Kim placed her hand over her forehead.

"God, I really am losing it."

"It's OK, you'll be fine. Hey you gonna drink that?" she asked, pointing to Kim's glass of tea she hadn't touched.

"Well.... I mean, you are technically, regardless.... cause.... well you know.... I'm.... I'm just gonna take this," she said, pulling the glass toward herself.

She began taking small sips.

Kim was sulking in the reality of her life. She was accustomed to feeling down and overwhelmed but she felt she had hit a new low.

"Hey, c'mon I don't wanna be lookin at that sad face from now on, you need to smile."

Kim ignored her.

"Ugh…. alright alright, what else? Tell me what else is on that pretty little head of yours. You got until the top of the hour. Whatever you wanna get off your chest, whatever you wanna ask, speak it now."

Kim shook her head in disbelief.

"Joey, I can't believe he's gone, and like that. I just feel really guilty about it. My father took his parents from him, in cold blood, right in front of him."

"K, I don't mean to point the finger but you do realize one-hundred percent of the people you've killed have families too, right?"

"I know, I know, it's a double standard. But for it to be Joey, it just feels different. I remember seeing him the first day I walked back into The Home. I'd known him from school but to see him there was just different. And to think he was there because..."

"Because your dad was doing his job, just like you've done yours for the past six years? You know, you're no saint but you've managed to find some actual compassion as of recently. Maybe you're not so heartless after all. Maybe I shouldn't be here."

Kim rolled her eyes.

"Listen, the sad truth of the matter is he's gone, but that's not your fault, you chose not to pull the trigger. And what your dad did years ago isn't your fault either. Don't let the actions of others manifest guilt in you, the only actions you have to atone for are your own. Remember that."

"But he put Joey in the same position I'm trying to keep Cindy out of..."

"But it's not your fault he ended up in it." Helena interrupted, "That happened like ten years ago, you found out this morning, how can it be your fault? Why should you feel guilty at all? Cut yourself a break Kim. You're harder on yourself than your boss at the office is. Live your life, control what you can control. You already beat yourself up for every little imperfection in your character but now you're beating yourself up over other people's imperfections too? You can't, you're you, nobody else. Be you, be Kim, take responsibility for Kim and her actions, no one else's. And above all else do what makes you happy, what feels right to you, what falls in line with what you want to accomplish."

Her tone was stern, direct, and commanding. It was different from what Kim had become used to coming out her mouth.

"You're gonna be fine Kim, you're a smart chick. I might've got your common sense but there's still at least half a brain in that head of yours," she smiled.

Kim tried to hide her own smile but it peeked out.

"Thanks," she whispered.

"Hey, I'm not just quick wit and good looks, I have my moments," she grinned.

Kim studied her for a moment.

"Then what are you?" she asked.

"What?"

"What are you?" she asked again.

"K, we've been over this," she laughed.

"So, you're really not real?"

"As far as reality is concerned, nah, you're sitting at this table talking to yourself right now."

"Great, twenty-six and I'm already losing my mind," Kim moaned.

"You're fine, don't trip. I promise you'll warm up to me."

"How long are you gonna be just showing up?" Kim asked.

Helena swished some tea around in her mouth thinking before she answered.

"Well, truthfully, that's kinda up to you. Remember I'm only here cause you chose to no longer bear your own emotions. Technically speaking once you decide to no longer be a heartless murder machine, I should disappear back into your mind. The fact that I'm still here now tells me you're not really considering quitting as much as you want everyone to believe. You haven't really set your mind on walking away or else I'd probably already be gone."

Kim stared at her curiously; how much she knew, how quickly she calculated things was incredible to her. Her ability to see through the things Kim said that weren't truly from her heart was remarkable. It was becoming more and more obvious they were connected in some way.

"I guess I'll sleep on it," she said standing from the table, "I think what's making the decision so hard for me is that I'm trying to please everyone. I mean, everyone in The Pool wants me to stay, but I feel like if I stay, I'm putting those I hold close at risk. It's also just getting tough to keep such a big secret from everyone."

Helena stood to her feet and walked around the table to Kim.

"This is Joy City. Everyone has secrets here and everyone does a fine job of keeping them while it still remains pretty obvious that nine outta ten people you pass by on the street have either killed someone, sold something illegal, stolen something, or committed some type of crime. You're doing fine keeping the secret, keep taking the precautions necessary and it'll stay just between the three of us."

"Three?" Kim asked.

"You, me, and Cindy."

Kim raised an eyebrow.

"Cindy doesn't know," Kim clarified.

Helena's head jerked back and she flashed Kim a concerned look. She then laughed under her breath and shook her head at Kim. She walked back around to the table and sat back down. She took a moment before speaking to gather her thoughts.

"Kim, what did you tell her today when you got home?" she asked.

"That I got caught in the crossfire of some gang stuff."

Helena had such a confused look on her face Kim got lost herself.

"And she believed that?" Helena asked.

Kim didn't answer, she just stood there

puzzled. She knew she wasn't done; she was waiting for her to continue.

Helena crossed her arms, "Kim, when you told her that.... what did she say?"

Helena's tone was soft, as though she were explaining something to a child.

"Ummm.... well she was lying down for bed when I walked in, so not much. She just said she was happy I was alright and that I could tell her the rest when I was ready."

"Mhmmm.... you could tell her the rest.... when you were ready?"

She spoke the words very slowly, making sure every syllable was justly pronounced.

"When you're ready.... to tell her the rest," Helena repeated.

Kim's eyes were locked directly on her, yet Helena would not make eye contact with her. As she spoke her eyes wandered all around the kitchen never stopping on Kim.

"Kim, you gave her the cover up excuse, what do you think she meant by *the rest*?" she asked.

She finally looked up at her squinting with a slight grin on her face. Kim's muscles tensed up, her stomach began to feel heavy, her mind analyzing every word she had spoken to Cindy as of recent, and every response she had given back.

"The girl's not dumb Kim," Helena added in a whisper.

Kim was staring into space, pondering everything. Trying to convince herself it wasn't so. *She couldn't* she thought.

"D-does she know..."

"Awww.... would you look at that," Helena interrupted gesturing towards the clock on the wall, "one o'clock, which means Q and A time is over. Sorry, maybe next time."

Kim's jaw dropped. Helena picked up the tea glasses from the table and placed them both in the sink. She turned around and walked right past Kim as she headed for the door.

"Goodnight babe, take it easy on that shoulder," she said.

She opened the door and stepped halfway out but stopped. She turned back around and looked directly at Kim. She was smiling that same perfect smile she had the day she first appeared.

"Talk to her Kim," she said, before disappearing out the door.

Kim's body felt stiff; she couldn't move. All she could do was hope. Hope she was wrong, hope Cindy had no clue, or hope she understood.

She crept back upstairs as quietly as she could, down the hallway, into her room, and under her covers.

Acknowledgements

I would like to dedicate the following page(s) to thank those that motivated me to keep writing, take a chance on my work, and push for publication. The following individuals were sent or given small excerpts of my work (not necessarily this one) and encouraged me to keep writing whether through their praise or constructive criticism.

Names listed in alphabetical order

Alexis Bright
Aliyah C.
Anna Thompson
Averry Cox
Ayana Reynolds
Brianna Watters
Britney Reynolds
Claire K.
Crane O'Hanlon
David L. Hawks
Erin Elledge
Hannah B. Brennan
Hannah Mokulis
Hephzibah Eniade
Hope Anderson
Izabella N. Vital

Kaliya Williams
Kelsee Piercy
Mackenzie Jolene & the entire Monahan family
Melissa Baez
Nichelle Dew
Nicole Nina Náray
Noor Khalid
Olivia Stephens
Peter Revel-Walsh
Rachel Grace Pigott
Regena Dossett
Romae Jarrett
Star Box
Tyson Hills
Whitney McMahan

I owe a special thanks to Vivien Reis, Jenna Moreci, and Bethany Atazadeh for the tips, advice, and coaching they provided via their Youtube channels. Without you three I could not have become the writer that I am today and the care of which this book was handled from start to finish resulting in the finished product would not be nearly as evident without the many teachings and guidance I received from each of you. Thank you all tremendously.

I owe a huge amount of gratitude to Mrs. Berkleigh Cirilli, one of my beta readers and the teacher who gave me the homework assignment that led to me finding my love for writing. Had it not been for you I probably would have never taken writing seriously and I would have never ended up discovering my love for storytelling. You were the first person to show belief in my writing ability and it means the world to me. Without you, not a word of any short story, novel, or narrative I have ever written would exist. As I have told you many times before I will never forget you, and thank you for everything.

A huge thanks to Zane Alexander for being one of my beta readers and assisting in marketing and exposure of my works. I really appreciate the encouragement and feedback you provided that ultimately let me know my work was good enough to be published. Your creativity and storytelling ability you showcase within your own works inspired me to push myself as I attempted to bring my works to life. And so, I absolutely must thank you for your contributions to this book's existence you may not have even known you made. Thank you Zane.

I must thank Samantha Dambach for all the help and resources she supplied me with to help transition my work from an idea in my head, to a word document on my laptop, to an eventual tangible book. Thank you so much for all the wisdom and knowledge you shared with me on the processes of writing, editing, and publishing. Know this book would not and could not exist today without your help.

To my amazing editor, Michelle Krueger, thank you so so so much. The editing process was something that initially terrified me and though we had some hiccups and slowdowns due to factors far out of either of our control we got through it together and ended up with a fantastic final copy of the book and I cannot thank you enough for that. Your edits, proofing, suggestions, praises, and criticisms were all immensely crucial in the polishing of this book and ultimately me achieving my dream of becoming a published author. Wherever it goes, know "The Joy City Pool" would not and could not be what it is today without you and your contributions to it. Thank you for everything.

Massive amount of thanks to Haze Long for bringing this book's front and back cover art to life. When I first sent you the front cover concept sketch that I did in color pencil I thought the cover would look pretty good but you and your talents made the cover truly great. Then you blew me away again with your incredible execution of the back cover. Looking over the finished product never ceases to amaze me and I'm truly honored to have pieces of your original artwork as my book's cover art. Thank you so much Haze.

And of course, I must thank my entire family for the love and support they showed me throughout the entire writing and publishing process.

I can't thank you all enough for the time and effort you sacrificed in contributing to this work. All the things each and every one of you did, told me you loved about my work, or told me you didn't like so much were considered and played a pivotal role in what the final product is today. I hope as you read you were able to take pride in knowing you contributed to this work in one way or another.

Finally, I want to thank any and all who picked up this novel and read it cover to cover. I truly hope you enjoyed your read.

Contact and Social Information

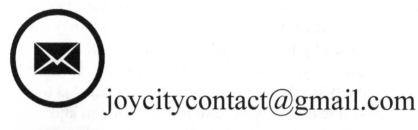 joycitycontact@gmail.com

 @EverythingJoyCity

 @Everything_JC

 @everythingjoycity